Also by Anthony McGowan:

The Donut Diaries

Einstein's Underpants
And How They Saved the World
(Shortlisted for the Roald Dahl Funny Prize 2010)

The Bare Bum Gang and the Holy Grail
The Bare Bum Gang and the Valley of Doom
The Bare Bum Gang and the Football Face-off
The Bare Bum Gang Battle the Dogsnatchers

For older readers:
Hellbent

Henry Tumour
(Winner of the Booktrust Teenage Prize 2006)
The Knife That Killed Me

THE DONUT DIARIES

of Dermot Milligan

REVENGE IS SWEET

As told by Anthony McGowan
Illustrated by David Tazzyman

CORGI

THE DONUT DIARIES: REVENGE IS SWEET
A CORGI BOOK 978 0 552 56439 7

Published in Great Britain by Corgi Books,
an imprint of Random House Children's Publishers UK
A Random House Group Company

This edition published 2012

3 5 7 9 10 8 6 4 2

The Random House Group Limited supports The Forest Stewardship Council® (FSC®),
the leading international forest-certification organisation. Our books carrying the FSC
label are printed on FSC®-certified paper. FSC is the only forest-certification scheme
supported by the leading environmental organisations, including Greenpeace. Our paper
procurement policy can be found at www.randomhouse.co.uk/environment

MIX
Paper from
responsible sources
FSC® C016897

Set in Bembo Regular 13pt/22pt

Corgi Books are published by Random House Children's Publishers UK,
61–63 Uxbridge Road, London W5 5SA

www.randomhousechildrens.co.uk
www.totallyrandombooks.co.uk
www.randomhouse.co.uk

Addresses for companies within The Random House Group Limited can be found at:
www.randomhouse.co.uk/offices.htm

THE RANDOM HOUSE GROUP Limited Reg. No. 954009

A CIP catalogue record for this book is available from the British Library.

Printed and bound by
CPI Group (UK) Ltd, Croydon, CRO 4YY

To Rosie, Gabriel and Rebecca,

who helped to make this.

The Bit Before The Story Really Gets Going

A new term is about to begin and everything
in the world is slightly less rubbish than it used
to be. My first term at St Michael's began at
the bottom and spiralled down from there, with
every kind of humiliation and embarrassment
being heaped on my chubby shoulders. I was
teased, bullied, goaded, mocked and shunned.
And not in a good way.

The main reason for this is that I was (and

am) a bit overweight. The main reason for *that* is that I eat too many donuts.

Do you need to know why I eat too many donuts? If you do, then frankly YOU'RE INSANE! Have you never rushed feverishly to the bakers or the supermarket or the donut stall, handed over your money with a shaking hand, snatched away the donut, hurried to a quiet corner and filled your mouth with its warm flesh like a tiger feasting on a hapless Indian villager? And while the lovely fluffy donut matter is in your mouth, you are happy, truly happy. As happy as a princess who has found her prince. Ah ...

NOTE TO SELF: NEVER AGAIN DESCRIBE YOURSELF AS A 'PRINCESS' UNLESS YOU DO ACTUALLY WANT TO LIVE THE REST OF YOUR LIFE IN UTTER MISERY.

So, no, you don't need a reason to eat too many donuts. You need a reason *not* to. And I've got that reason. I can see it now when I look down: a belly that bulges and tries to escape out of my shirt, like some cheesy monster from an old science fiction movie. I keep thinking a woman in a hat is going to point at it and scream, 'It's horrible! It's horrible!' and then faint.

That's my dilemma. I love donuts, but I know they're turning me into a joke. A fat joke. So my goal for this term is to cut down to one donut a day. Except in emergencies. Or special occasions. Or if I'm celebrating some unusual triumph. Or if something rotten has happened and I need to be cheered up. Or if I need to turn to the Sweet Donut of Forgiveness because I've done something bad.

Being the fat kid is always a challenge. You

need guts and determination to pull it off. But add being the fat kid to the already traumatic experience of starting at a new school and you've got a recipe for disaster. Last term, my persecutor-in-chief was the evil Floppy-Haired Kid (or FHK), whose real name is Steerforth and

who has a mind as cunning as a weasel with a PhD from the University of Sly. His speciality is appearing friendly whilst secretly stabbing you in the back. He quite often then stabs you in the front as well.

But he who laughs last gets the last laugh (or whatever the saying is), and I got my revenge. The revenge involved a plan that was just as ingenious and sly and evil as any ever cooked up by the FHK. But even though it was evil, it wasn't, you know, Evil, because *I'm* a goody and *he's* a baddy. Plus it concluded with him getting a big dollop of monkey poo in the face, which is absolutely the best way for a plan to end. In fact, any plan which doesn't end in the bad guy getting a face-full of monkey poo should consider itself a failure.*

* It was, in fact, chimpanzee poo, but for some reason monkey poo sounds funnier to me.

In all this I was helped by my new friends, Renfrew, Spam and Corky. Renfrew looks more like a rodent than some creatures that are actually members of the rodent family. Spam is a skinny giant, like a daddy-long-legs that's been gigantified by a gigantifying ray.* Corky has a stutter so bad he sounds like someone making fun of someone else with a stutter. But a fat kid really couldn't wish for three better friends.

I began writing my diary because it was part of the treatment plan invented for

---

* Such rays remain in the realm of science fiction, but I reckon that sooner or later one will be invented, so you could super-size your own McDonalds without having to pay extra. You could also use it to take over the world.

me by a gruesome nutritionist
called Doc Morlock. I was
supposed to write down
how many donuts I ate every
day and, what's even worse,
my 'feelings' about things. It's
difficult to explain to someone

like Doc Morlock
that as I'm a boy
rather than a girl I
don't really have feelings.
What I have are moods.
Failure to comply meant
being sent to the dreaded
Camp Fatso. Camp Fatso is
where fat kids are sent to be
tortured with gruel and cross-
country runs.

Well, mainly because of my brilliant Evil Plan – I mean evil plan – I managed to avoid getting sent to Camp Fatso. But it still hovers over me like the shadow of Something Really Bad . . .

Monday 8 January

I walked in through the school gates on the first
day of the new term a bit less terrified than I'd
been on my first day of the first term. My mates
were already there in a huddle, sheltering from
the icy January wind. That wind felt a lot like
when you're in the bath and your horrible sister
bursts in and pours freezing water down your
back just because you put a firework up her
teddy's bum and blew the stuffing out of it.

NOTE TO SELF: ALWAYS
REMEMBER TO LOCK THE
BATHROOM DOOR AFTER
YOU'VE BLOWN UP ONE OF
RUBY'S CUDDLY TOYS.

'Hey, Donut!' they all
shouted with one voice (my
friends, I mean, not Ruby's cuddly
toys, who talk to her and nobody else,
and do it in teeny-weeny voices that only
Ruby and the pixies can hear).

'Hey, guys,' I said.

They were talking about what they'd got for
Christmas. Spam's parents are pretty rich, so he'd
got an iPad. Renfrew's mum and dad don't believe
in technology so he'd ended up with a violin,
which we all found pretty funny, although not as

funny as it would have been if he'd got a tuba.

I was actually rather nervous about this whole topic of conversation, for the very good reason that what I'd got for Christmas was a skipping rope.

That's right.

A piece of rope that you use for the purpose of skipping.

I'd been given a skipping rope for two reasons:

1) I could use it to skip with, thereby contributing to my Healthier Lifestyle.
2) I didn't deserve anything decent

because I'd blown up Ruby's teddy.

It was Renfrew who asked the fatal question, probably trying to deflect everyone from making fun of his violin.

'What did you get, Donut?'

All the faces swivelled towards me. I tried to think of something believable – some sort of gadget – but my mind went blank. I couldn't think of anything. I started to panic. Sweat broke out on my forehead. The image of the skipping rope swung in front of my eyes. And then I was saved. Well, sort of saved. Like when you get saved from being eaten by a shark because a killer whale eats you first, which is frankly the very worst way of getting saved.

'Hello.'

It was my arch-enemy, my nemesis, Steerforth,

the Floppy-Haired Kid himself. He was flanked by a couple of his cronies, who always followed him, the way a noxious burp follows a bad burger.

I looked him straight in the eye. He was smirking. He was nearly always smirking. They should make signs that say 'NO SMIRKING' instead of 'NO SMOKING' and you could hold them up whenever he walked by. Sadly, I didn't have one now.

NOTE TO SELF: LOOK ON THE INTERNET FOR A CHEAP 'NO SMIRKING' SIGN.

'I suppose you're thinking that the worst is over for you, my plump chum?' He spoke in such a sweet tone you'd really think that he was my chum, unless you knew him. 'Got through the first term unscathed, plain sailing from now on, eh?'

I shrugged. There was no point in getting into a war of words with the FHK. He was always going to win it. Unless you fought back with the kind of ammo that comes out of a monkey's bum.*

'But the thing is, my donut-munching *compadre*' – and here he stepped towards me and took hold of my cheeks with his fingers – 'it *is*. It really is. I've been thinking that I was acting like an idiot last term. It's time for us both to move on. I don't suppose we'll ever be friends, and that saddens me a little. But at least we can be civilized acquaintances.'

And then he slid smoothly away, like a wet fart.

I turned to the others, who were all staring.

I shrugged.

* See earlier note about monkey poo. This seems to apply even more to monkey bums.

They shrugged.

Sometimes, in life, shrugging is all you can do.

As it was the first day back after the holidays we were all a bit, er, high-spirited at morning registration, and our form teacher, Mr Wells, who normally tries to be everyone's best friend, got into a right old state. I felt a bit sorry for him, but not so much that I didn't join in with the paper aeroplane throwing, animal-noise making, Chinese burning, etc. etc.

Oh, in case you don't know, 'Chinese burning' doesn't mean burning Chinese people, which would be wrong and racist, and also stupid as they have a massive army and would totally destroy you. No, it's when you grab someone's wrists with both your hands and twist the skin in opposite directions, causing Immense Agony to the person you're torturing.

Except me, that is. For some freakish reason I'm immune to Chinese burns. I've got a feeling that one day this will save my life, but for now it's only useful when I challenge people like Renfrew to a Chinese burn-athon, as it guarantees my victory.

NOTE TO SELF: SEND LETTER TO MI5, MI6, BRITISH NAVAL INTELLIGENCE, ETC. ETC., TELLING THEM ABOUT MY SPECIAL ABILITY TO WITHSTAND CHINESE BURNS IN CASE IT CAN BE OF SERVICE TO THE NATION.

DONUT COUNT:

It's the first day back so I reckon I'm allowed the extra half, OK?

Tuesday 9 January

Disaster. Because of yesterday's hi-jinks, Mr Wells has changed how we sit. We now have to go boy-girl-boy-girl.* This is the worst thing that

* Technically, as there are 32 of us, we go: boy-girl-boy-girl-boy-girl-boy-girl-boy-girl-boy-girl-boy-girl-boy-girl-boy-girl-boy-girl-boy-girl-boy-girl-boy-girl-boy-girl-boy-girl. Hmmm, I think that might be the most boring thing I've ever written in this diary. Possibly the most boring thing ever written by anyone in any diary in history. And going on about it makes it even more boring.

has happened to me since I was old enough to realize that I had sisters.

On one side of me I have Tamara Bello, who'd be a dead cert to play the princess who could feel a pea even though she was sleeping on ten mattresses. By which I mean she's quite pretty, in a princessy kind of way, but also a royal pain in the bum.

On the other side of me I have this girl called Ludmilla Pfumpf. Her real name isn't Pfumpf – that's just the sound she makes whenever she stands up or sits down. I've concealed her real name to avoid giving offence. Ludmilla Pfumpf has bulldog jowls and weightlifter arms and she smells of meat. You'd have to be a meat expert to say for definite what kind of meat she smells of, but I'd guess it's probably buffalo. Or maybe horse. Possibly badger. Imagine wandering into

a butcher's that specialized in buffalo, horse and badger meat and you wouldn't be far off target in terms of the smell. Now, smelling of meat is only the ninth worst thing you could smell of – coming after poo, wee, vomit, blue cheese, belly-button gunk, my dad's feet, dog spit and a tramp's underpants – but it still isn't a smell you'd choose to sit next to.

Apart from her 'Pfumpf' noise, Ludmilla doesn't say very much, but I could hear her stomach rumbling all day, and I lived in mortal fear that she was going to raise her chunky buttock – as knotted and knobbly as a bag of walnuts – and pump out a badger-flavoured fart in my direction.

I made the mistake of telling my family about it at tea time, thinking it would make a funny story. My dad seemed to enjoy it but Mum said it wasn't nice to mock the afflicted, and that it wasn't Ludmilla's fault that she had a bum like a bag of walnuts. But then my psycho sisters, Ruby (who wears pink) and Ella (who wears black), decided that I must fancy Ludmilla, and was going to go out with her and probably get married and we'd have mutant, meat-smelling babies together, etc. etc. etc.

DONUT COUNT:

See – I'm being good, I really am, despite the whole Ludmilla provocation.

Wednesday 10 January

As part of my campaign to cut down (a bit) on donuts, I've started to eat a lot of bananas. This isn't as bad as it sounds. I like bananas. Most other fruit basically counts as work – I always feel like I need a lie down after an orange or an apple. I once ate a mango and had to stay in bed for the whole weekend to get over it. All fruit other than bananas I eat as a favour to my mum, to make her feel like she's being a proper parent. But eating a banana, well, it's quite nice, isn't it? Not *donut* nice, of course, but then nothing is donut nice except donuts.

The funny thing is that I don't like things that are banana-*flavoured* – you know, those weird banana-flavoured toffees, or banana milk-shakes. In fact, I hate all banana-flavoured things except for actual bananas themselves. Cherries are the opposite. Real cherries, you know, off *trees*, don't really taste of anything as far as I can tell, but cherry-flavoured sweets are delicious, probably because they don't have any actual cherry in them. They ought to get the stuff that makes cherry-flavoured sweets so delicious and squirt it into cherries. Then you'd have cherry-flavoured cherries, and I'd eat them till I burst.

But in the absence of cherry-flavoured cherries, I take a banana to school to have as an emergency snack, in case I get tempted by a donut. Actually, quite often I'll have a banana *and* a donut, but in those circumstances the banana has probably saved me from eating two donuts, so it's still done its job. In that situation – I mean eating a banana *and* a donut – the key is to eat the banana before the donut, not after it. That way you get a rising level of sugary goodness, like this:

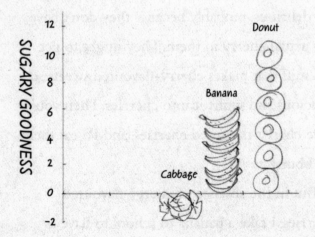

(I added in cabbage because the graph looked a bit silly and unprofessional with just two columns in it.)

If you eat the donut first and the banana afterwards, then you get this much less satisfactory result:

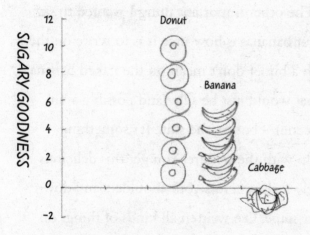

I think you'll agree that the evidence is conclusive. The graph clearly shows that eating a banana after a donut will leave you feeling sadly let down, and if you do it too often you will get stuck thinking that everything in life will always be disappointing, and that way you'll probably have a rubbish life and end up as a tramp or working in a butcher's shop slicing up badgers and horses for a living.

The other important thing I wanted to say about bananas is how nice it is to write on them with a biro. I don't mean on the naked banana – that would just be silly (and possibly a bit obscene) – but on the skin. It's something to do with the texture. You get this delicious tingly feeling across your shoulders and down your spine. I've written all kinds of things on bananas, including '*Twilight* is a load of old rubbish' (to annoy Ella) and 'Pink is poo' (to annoy Ruby).

Today I doodled a shark's
mouth.

I showed it to Renfrew, who sits
in front of me now, and made a sort of
growling noise.

Without even looking at me, Tamara
Bello said, 'Oh, so sharks growl, do they?'
which made me feel about this big (I'm
demonstrating this by stretching out my thumb
and forefinger).

It's always rubbish being corrected on shark
facts by a girl. If there's one thing that ought
to be true in the universe it's that boys should
know more about sharks than girls. I mean, how
would she like it if I started telling her about, er,
dresses and flowers and how to make people feel
this (I'm doing that thing with my finger and
thumb again) small?

Of course, I should have come back with a witty reply. Or at least I should have pointed out that I knew very well that sharks don't growl, that growling is limited to land-based predators and my stomach after more than four hours without a donut. I should have explained that it was a joke, that the fact that sharks don't growl was *exactly* why I made my banana-shark growl. I should have yelled in her face:

'IT'S CALLED INCONGRUITY, DUMMY, WHICH IS WHEN YOU PUT TWO THINGS THAT DON'T BELONG TOGETHER TO TRY TO GET A LAUGH.'

But the thing is, I'm slightly afraid of Tamara Bello, so I settled for just acting embarrassed and flustered, which I'm sure really taught *her* a lesson.

I don't know if it's just paranoia, but it seemed

that whenever I happened to look up today I found myself staring into the face of the Floppy-Haired Kid. In the corridors, in the dinner hall, in the schoolyard – he was always there. And when he saw me looking he'd break out into this big smile, as if he was actually pleased to see me. Most unnerving.

DONUT COUNT:

Steady as she goes!

Thursday 11 January

I suppose it was only a matter of time before I
did something to ruin my life. At least I managed
to get through THREE WHOLE DAYS without
proving myself to be an ASS OF TITANIC
PROPORTIONS. Strange that only yesterday
I was a happy schoolboy without a care in the
world, except for the fact that I was a bit too fat
and had to sit next to someone who smelled of
meat, and that I lived with two psychologically

disturbed sisters and a dad who spent all his time in the toilet and a mum who was screwed up in at least eight different ways.

It all began with my banana. And now I'm thinking that perhaps all bad things begin with a banana. In fact, I reckon it wasn't an apple that Eve gave to Adam in the Garden of Eden, but a banana. And then there was ... well, OK, I can't think of any other bad things that began with a banana. But today I realized that bananas are just slyly lulling you into a false sense of security by being quite nice to eat and draw on.

Anyway, at breakfast this morning I was in the kitchen. I was having the normal breakfast conversation with Mum. You know how it goes:

MUM: What have you got on today?
ME: Stuff.

MUM: I mean, what lessons?

ME: The usual.

That sort of thing. Why do mums and dads always pretend that they care about what you've done or what you're going to do? I mean, I don't ask them what *they've* been up to. What if they actually started *telling* me? It'd be terrible . . . because, frankly, who cares?

And while Mum was grilling me, I was, as usual, doodling on my banana with a biro. Didn't even think about it. Yesterday it was a shark, today it would be something else. It wasn't even really conscious. It was like one of those tunes you don't realize you've been whistling until someone thumps you and tells you to 'STOP THE HECK WHISTLING YOU ANNOYING FAT KID.'

I chucked the banana in my bag along with all the other stuff I needed for school.

Nothing too terrible happened until morning break. It was raining like the end of the world, so we had to stay in our form rooms. Mr Wells was still in a bad mood from the other day, so he said we had to read quietly to ourselves. My book was in the bottom of my bag. I'm reading *The Lord of the Rings* for the eighth time. It's probably a record. It's a real shame that reading *The Lord of the Rings* isn't an Olympic sport because I'd definitely get a medal – probably gold.

So I had to dig down through all the other crud in my bag – PE kit, textbooks, sweet wrappers, etc. etc. Everything I took out, I put on my desk. Including the banana.

Now remember, on one side of me I've got Tamara Bello, reading her book of Russian short stories, and on the other side there's Ludmilla Pfumpf, reading *Badger Butchery for Dummies*.

It was only then that what I'd actually doodled on the banana suddenly dawned on me. I'd been thinking about how much I love bananas. So I'd written: *I Love You*, and drawn a little heart.

And now I'd just put this banana love letter on my desk. Right in front of Tamara Bello. No, not banana love *letter*. Banana love BOMB.

My mind slowed down. I saw Tamara's head begin to turn. She was slowly focusing in on the

stuff on my desk. On the banana. She was going to think that I'd written it for her. That I loved not my banana, but Tamara Bello.

I reached out. My movements were thick and clumsy. Still she turned. Her eyes were dipping towards the yellow horror. Already I could see the slightly puzzled look on her gruesomely perfect face.

I grabbed at the banana. But it was more like the flapping of a sea lion. I might as well have been using one of Mr Fricker's false hands. And

so my grab turned into a scoop, which turned into a slap, which sent the offending banana zipping across my desk and right into the lap of Ludmilla Pfumpf.

Ludmilla put down her book on badger butchery and stared at the thing that had landed in her lap. She put her hand down, and at the same time I reached out for the banana. My fingers accidentally stroked hers as I fumbled around for a grip. Then we both had hold of the banana. She looked up at me, her face like a confused rhino's. And then we both pulled. Had she read the message? Did she just want the banana? I couldn't tell.

People had begun to sense the kerfuffle. They were looking round. Renfrew was staring at me. So was Spam. Mr Wells glanced up from his newspaper. It was getting out of control. I needed that banana. Ludmilla's arm was stretched out, exposing the one vulnerable spot in her tough, scaly hide. I sent my free hand out on a deadly dangerous mission. It found her armpit, huge and moist. It tickled. Her great crusty face wrinkled. A strangely girlish giggle escaped her lips and she let go of the banana.

But I was not yet safe.

Mr Wells was beginning to speak.

'Give me that . . .' he began.

This was terrible. He was going to take the banana. Read the banana. Quite possibly read it *out loud* to the class. I had to act fast. There was only one thing to do.

I opened my mouth.

I raised the banana to my lips.

I bit.

Ever eaten a banana, skin and all?

I guess not.

It wasn't nice. I can't say it was the worst thing I've ever eaten – they've given us many worse things for school lunch – but it wasn't the sort of thing I ever wanted to have in my mouth again.

Of course the class went insane, yelling and screaming and making puke noises. Mr Wells never finished his sentence. What could he say? It's not like there was a school rule against eating bananas in their skins during break time.

In three savage bites I finished the thing. Then I sat back and burped. A few of the guys cheered.

Tamara Bello gave me a very strange look. At the time I wasn't sure if it was because she'd seen what was written on the banana or because of the whole grossness of what had followed.

I didn't even dare look at Ludmilla.

I told my dad the story of the Banana of Doom this evening. I told him it because I was in the downstairs toilet, writhing around in agony, and he was outside wanting to know how long I'd be in there. I was writhing around in agony because the banana skin I'd so rashly eaten was launching an escape bid.

When I finished telling him (it took me a while because I was doing quite a lot of groaning and moaning) I heard a strange sort of wheezing sound coming through the door.

It took me a few seconds to work out that he was laughing.

DONUT COUNT:

Well, can you blame me? Under the circumstances I thought it was quite restrained.

Friday 12 January

I knew it was going to be bad. And it was. Bad,
I mean. On the Higgenthorpe Badness Scale,
which goes up to 13, it would definitely reach a
creditable 11.6 by the end of the day.

It began as I came through the school gates.
Banana skins rained down on me, like . . . well,
there's nothing much you could compare it with,
although being hit with a banana skin hurts
about as much as being hit in the face with a
small fish. It's more humiliating than painful.

I looked around to see if the Floppy-Haired Kid was behind it, but there was no sign of him. Then a mean prefect called Ivan the Terrible turned up and yelled at me to pick up the mess, which was totally adding insult to injury. Last term I accidentally head-butted Ivan in the nuts, and that had somewhat biased him against me. But even before that he was known as a brutal bully, hence his nickname, Flowery Doris.*

But that only raised the Higgenthorpe Badness rating up to 6, which is not far from my usual background levels.

At morning break Tamara Bello came up to me.

* That's just a joke, by the way. Ivan the Terrible was, of course, the nickname of the prefect whose real name was Ivan Szymanowski. And right there you see another good reason to call him 'the Terrible', as nobody on Earth knows how to pronounce Szymanowski.

She had a serious expression on her face, as though she was about to announce that I had a terminal disease and had only three weeks to live. I had to remind myself that she was just a twelve-year-old schoolgirl and not a world expert on fatal and probably embarrassing diseases.

'I appreciate your sentiments,' she said, still with that terminal-disease face.

'What?'

'I mean, I understand what you were trying to say.'

'Eh?'

'On your banana.'

'I wasn't trying to say anything. It was just—'

'But I'm afraid you're not my type.'

'Oh, I know I'm not your type. You're not my type *either*. I don't even *have* a type. I was—' My voice was getting higher and higher as I spoke – it was lucky that Tamara interrupted me before I reached the sort of range only audible to bats.

'And I understand why you're now pretending that it was all a big misunderstanding, although I think it's rather shoddy to declare your feelings like that and then act like you hadn't. Try again when you've grown up a bit.'

Then she wheeled away, leaving me with my mouth hanging open.

Bad, you say, but surely not quite an 11.6 on the Higgenthorpe Badness Scale?

Well, the Badness hadn't finished with me yet.

Lunch was some kind of pie. There was literally no way of knowing what kind of pie. Some sort of brown stuff. You'd think that must mean it was a meat pie of some kind – maybe one of Ludmilla's badgers – but it actually tasted more like cheese.

Brown cheese? Is there such a thing in the world?

Anyway, afterwards I was sitting on a bench in the yard, trying not to remember the pie, although it was a bit like when someone screams at you out of the blue: 'Don't think about an elephant!'

Spam, Renfrew and Corky were with me, and they were all equally traumatized by the brown cheese incident. Then, suddenly, there was a *pfumpf* noise, and a smell of horseflesh. You know how in a war film there's always a bit where a mortar shell lands in the middle of a group of Nazis, and they go flying off, arms and legs flailing? Well, it was a bit like that now. Renfrew and the other guys exploded out of there. But I couldn't move. I couldn't move because Ludmilla was sitting on the bumflap of my blazer. I thought about slipping out of the blazer and just leaving it there, like lizards that can shed their tails, but I was sort of paralysed.

I turned slowly to look into the huge face of Ludmilla Pfumpf. Her tiny black eyes, set deep between her jutting brows and the massive fleshy expanse of her cheeks, were drilling into me. And her mouth . . . her *mouth*. It was doing something. It had bent itself into a strange shape, hitherto unseen except in nightmares. Her *teeth*. I could see her teeth. They were small and white, like tic-tacs. Small teeth in large faces have always frightened me.

And now she was reaching into her clothing.

OMG.

What was she doing? She was rummaging, feeling for something. Something nestled into her armpit. And now she was drawing it out, that horrific 'smile' (if smile it was) still caught on her face, like a dead kangaroo stuck on a barbed-wire fence. The hand gripping whatever it was that she'd concealed under her clothing was free now. She stretched it out towards me. I looked down. And there, clutched in that massive fist, was a bag of chips: greasy, steaming, fetid.

I tried to speak, but nothing would come out. I shook my head.

'*Hhhhhhggggghhh*,' said Ludmilla.

It was too much for me. She was just too powerful. I put my trembling fingers into her bag and took out a chip. It was still hot, although whether the heat was left over from the frying or had been imparted by her armpit, I couldn't say. And then, my hand still trembling, I put the chip to my mouth, and ate. I was dimly aware of

a sort of groan, which must have come from my companions.

Then Ludmilla nodded, satisfied, and stood up.

'Bye,' she said, in a voice that rumbled like an earthquake. I think it was the first actual word I'd ever heard her utter. Then she thumped away on her tree-trunk legs.

My friends rematerialized.

'Thanks for backing me up there, guys,' I complained.

Spam ignored my sarcasm. 'Do you realize what you've done?' he said.

'What? Nothing, I didn't do anything.'

'The chip,' intoned Renfrew. 'You took a chip from her.'

'And then you ate it,' added Spam.

'So . . . ? That doesn't mean anything, does it? It was only a chip.'

'Among her people it does,' said Spam. 'It means a lot. It has grave significance.'

'Her people . . . ?' He'd made it sound as if she was a member of a lost tribe or alien race.

'The Pfumpfs. You're one of *them* now.'

I put my head in my hands and groaned.

I could see the truth of it. Whether I wanted to be or not, I was now a Pfumpf.

DONUT COUNT:

No matter how bad things get, I'm determined to make up for yesterday's lapse. Four days of half-rations and I'll be back on course.

Saturday 13 January/
Sunday 14 January

That image – the one of Ludmilla reaching
into her armpit and pulling out a bag of chips
– haunted me all weekend, ruining everything,
the way someone else's eggy fart can ruin a really
good movie.

Actually there were plenty of other things
to ruin the weekend, such as Dad having one of
his bad days on Saturday. He refused to come
out of the toilet at all, and Mum had to feed

him bits of grilled bacon which she slid under the door. Then, on Saturday evening, Ruby did one of her famous screams that goes on for two hours. I don't mean, like, five minutes. I mean an actual two hours. All I'd done was borrow her iPod. And very slightly break it. Served her right for having so much rubbish music on it. And anyway, you have to expect things to get slightly broken eventually, don't you? I mean, nothing lasts for ever, does it? And if things did, then all the people in China who make things would be out of a job and probably starve to death in their gazillions. Was that what Ruby wanted? Dad could probably have fixed it, but he was in the toilet making a sound a bit like the song of the humpback whale, probably in an attempt to drown out Ruby's screams.

Then, on Saturday night, the weirdest thing of all happened, although I'm not sure if it counts as good or bad. One minute me and Mum and Ruby were watching the telly (Dad was still in the toilet, though all was nice and quiet in there as he'd stopped his whale singing). And then, suddenly, I sensed that there were other entities present in the room. I felt the hair on the back of my neck stand up, and I had a strong urge to run and hide.

Mum and Ruby felt it too, and together we all turned towards the door. Two thin figures stood there. One was immensely tall. They were both dressed entirely in black, although their faces were deathly pale.

'This is Crow,' said the slighter of the two, who I now recognized as my sister Ella. 'He's my boyfriend.'

Crow made a small movement with his right index finger. It was as long as a pencil and tipped with a black nail, sharpened to a point. Crow's black hair came down to his shoulders and looked like it had been varnished. For a second I thought he was wearing a cloak, but it was just a long black coat.

At that moment I heard a tremendous flush from the toilet, and a second later Dad emerged from the downstairs loo. His shirt was out, his hair was ruffled and he hadn't shaved for a couple of days. He stared at Crow and Crow stared back at him. It was like two completely different species of animal coming across each other in the jungle.

'Me and Crow are just going to listen to some music,' said Ella.

'Not in your bedroom you're not,' said Mum,

emerging from her trance. 'You can come in here and I'll make a pot of tea.'

'I'm not staying in here with a bunch of stupid goths,' said Ruby, and flounced out, pinkly.

I stayed on, and witnessed what was probably the most embarrassing half-hour in the history of the world. Mum and Dad sat on the sofa. Crow sat on a chair while Ella perched on the arm. She held onto one of his ridiculously long fingers.

Actually, come to think of it, only his index finger was abnormal. It reminds me of something . . . can't think what . . . No, wait, it's that freaky little creature – hang on – just going to look it up on the internet . . .

Right, back again – it's called an aye-aye, and it has just one scary long finger that it uses to

pull grubs out of holes in trees. And it says this
about it on Wiki:

> The aye-aye is often viewed as a harbinger of
> evil and killed on sight. Others believe that if
> it points its narrow middle finger at someone,
> they are condemned to death. Some say the
> appearance of an aye-aye in a village predicts the
> death of a villager, and the only way to prevent
> this is to kill it. The Sakalava people go so far
> as to claim that aye-ayes sneak into houses
> through their thatched roofs and murder the
> sleeping occupants by using their middle finger to
> puncture the victim's aorta.

All *very* significant, I think you'll agree.

Anyway, Mum kept asking Crow questions
like 'Milk and sugar?' and 'What GCSEs are you

doing?' and 'What would you like to do when you grow up?'

Crow would only answer by moving that huge finger – side to side for 'no', up and down for 'yes', and some complex system of wiggles for 'Chemistry, Physics, English, Maths' or 'chief henchman for Nosferatu, Lord of the Undead'.

You could see Mum getting more and more annoyed. Dad just looked like he wanted to get back to his toilet, but was hanging on for the Good of the Family.

In the end I couldn't take any more of it and went to read my chemistry textbook in bed.

Yeah, that's how bad it was.

When I woke up on Sunday morning I checked for puncture marks on my jugular. Nothing so far, but Crow could just be playing a clever game.

DONUT COUNT:

A struggle, but I managed it. Maybe I have
conquered the demon?

Monday 15 January

Well, that was definitely one weird day.

Where to begin?

In the school toilets, I suppose.

So, what was I doing in the school toilets at 10.15 a.m., right in the middle of the Battle of Hastings?*

Well, there were two reasons for that. The

* It wasn't, of course, the real Battle of Hastings, but the Battle of Hastings as taught by Mr Wells, who is our history teacher as well as our form teacher.

first was to do with the new high-fibre diet
I'd been put on by my mum in alliance with
my nutritionist, the dastardly Dr Morlock. I
was putting away a lot of Shredded Wheat,
baked beans, brown bread, carrots, cabbage, the
occasional wholemeal donut and, of course,
bananas. And all that fibre eventually turns into
a lot of wind. Which would have been fine,
normally. A well-timed classroom fart can get
you major brownie points e.g. just as the teacher
stands up or sits down, or in the silence after
they've asked a particularly tricky question. The
key is to make it loud enough for your mates
to hear, but just below the level at which it
becomes audible to the teacher.

Of course, I wasn't the best farter in the class.
That accolade went to Corky, who could
literally make his farts talk. But I was a reliable

guy to have around when Corky's bomb-bay
was empty.

But that was no use now because of the new
seating arrangements. I just couldn't freely pump
one out when I was forced to sit next to Tamara
Bello. It simply wouldn't be right. It would
be like farting on the Queen. And then there
was the Ludmilla Pfumpf issue on the other
side. What if she took it as some kind of secret
message? A gaseous serenade, following up my
banana love letter?

We weren't allowed to go to the bog during
lessons, so I put my hand up and told Mr Wells
that I'd left my asthma inhaler in my coat pocket,
and that I needed it now because I was having
an attack. Like all the best lies, it had an element
of truth in it. My asthma inhaler *was* in my coat
pocket. But I wasn't having an attack. Or not

66

an attack of asthma, anyway, just wind, which
I suppose is the opposite of asthma. Asthma is
when you can't *get* air in, and farting is when
you can't *keep* it in.

Mr Wells tutted but said yes – on the grounds
of not wanting to get sued if I died, I expect.

I didn't go to the cloakroom but to the toilet,
thinking that was a more civilized place to
break wind. Of course, as soon as I got there I
didn't need to fart any more, which is the *perfect*
definition of irony. Still, I thought I'd better hang
around in case the urge came back.

And that's why I was sitting in the cubicle
reading the graffiti on the wall.

If you believe in
time travel, meet me here
last Thursday.

Yeah, very funny.

I'd given up on the fart when I heard the door to the loos creak open. It was a curiously stealthy sound, not at all like the usual CRASH you get when a kid bursts in. That made me think it must be a teacher on the lookout for skivers.

I'll admit I panicked a bit. I suppose I could have said that I'd just popped into the toilet on my way back from the cloakroom, but it wouldn't have looked good. So I pulled my legs up to hide them from whoever was out there.

I heard some light steps and then a soft noise, a bit like the sound you get in the dining hall when the dinner lady flops a dollop of disgusting mashed potato on your plate. Then more steps, and the door opening and closing again.

I waited a minute then came out of the

cubicle. There was something on the floor. It took me a moment to realize what it was.

A poo.

Yep. A genuine glistening brown poo.

I shook my head in disbelief. Someone had actually come into the toilet and pooped on the floor.

I wondered if I should clean it up, but that was just too gross. Anyway, he who did the crime should do the time. I also thought about reporting the incident. But then I'd have to explain why I was in there. So I stepped over the offending object and ran back to class.

I went back to check out the crime scene when the bell rang for lunch. There was quite a commotion. The door was blocked by a piece of tape, and a couple of prefects were standing guard. A little crowd had gathered. I asked a kid called Spinks, who I sort of know, what was going on.

'Someone dumped on the floor. Then a prefect stepped in it. He's had to go to hospital.'

'Just for stepping in some . . . ?'

'He slipped. Broke his ankle, apparently.'

'Which one?'

'His right one.'

'No, I mean which prefect?'

'Oh. Ivan the Terrible.'

'Good.'

At that moment, the door opened and the school caretaker, Mr Aziz, came out carrying

a yellow plastic bag with DANGEROUS WASTE
MATERIALS written on it. He looked like he was
carrying an unexploded bomb.

'This is not my job,' he grumbled as he went
past.

I told the guys about it over lunch (it was
fishcakes, although you couldn't find any actual
fish in them – just a fishy flavour, as if a haddock
had burped on some potatoes).

'Maybe someone just couldn't make it to the
can,' said Spam, who usually tried to see the best
in people.

'Nah – it wasn't like that. This person *crept* in
– they weren't dashing.'

'Sh-sh-sh,' said Corky.

'So it was just some kind of gross-out stunt,
then?' said Renfrew, shaking his head.

'Sh–sh–sh,' said Corky.

'Yeah, guess so,' I said. 'It's just that . . .'

'Sh–sh–sh,' said Corky.

'Or a message of some kind?' asked Renfrew.

'Funny way to leave a message,' I said.

'Like writing on a banana?' Renfrew smiled.

'Shut up,' I said, and slapped the back of his head.

'Sh–sh–shocking,' said Corky.

DONUT COUNT:

Easy!

Tuesday 16 January

The banana incident still haunts me. Haunts me in the sense of biting me on the bum and not letting go, which I admit is a non-standard way of getting haunted.

It was there on my desk this morning.

Six inches long and gently curved.

No, not another poo, but a banana. On it someone had written:

Or rather, the words had been scratched into the banana skin with some sharp implement and the scars dyed with red ink.

I looked over at Ludmilla.

She smiled back at me and gave a little wave, wiggling her fingers. I noticed that one of the fingers had a plaster on it.

And I realized what she'd done.

She'd written the message in blood.

I thought I was going to puke up my Weetabix.

Then, at break, something happened that took me back to the bad old days of last term. Well, sort of . . .

I was hanging out with the guys as usual. Spam had just come up with one of his Amazing Facts.

'Over the past four hundred years,' he'd said, 'over a million people have been killed by tigers.'

That took some absorbing. If it was invented, then it was a nice piece of work. If it was true, then it played uneasily with my deep-rooted fear of being eaten. I'd always reckoned that a bear would get me, but if the figure of a million tiger victims was true, it made it more than likely that the big stripy cat would be the one to Feast On My Flesh.

I was thinking about this when I caught sight of something out of the corner of my eye. A gang, made up mainly of the cool kids from Xavier House plus a few of the swots from Campion, was approaching us in a very peculiar manner. It took me a few seconds to work out what was going on. At first I thought they were supposed to be some kind of giant beetle. Then it struck me: they were pretending to row a boat. They must have practised because it was pretty realistic. You could tell that the sea was quite rough, and the boat was being tossed about. One kid was standing at the prow, and he was pretending to hold something – something long and spear-like. This kid, whose name was Nick Fedallah, then pointed towards our bench.

'Thar she blows!' he yelled, and the 'boat' changed course towards me.

Then I got it. It was a whaling expedition, and I was the whale. Sort of quite funny, really.

If you weren't me.

When they got closer, Fedallah hurled his harpoon.

'Strike!' he yelled. 'I got me a big one! Let's reel him in, boys, reel him in.'

Then they all hauled on the imaginary rope.

Of course, by now the whole schoolyard was enjoying the spectacle. It's not often, after all, that you get to watch an authentic whale-slaying at break time. Mrs Smote, the simple-minded playground monitor, who wore wellington boots and a coat made out of cat pelts (you could still see their little ears and the blank, leathery eye-sockets), laughed and clapped like she was at the circus.

I wasn't quite sure what to do. Should I just ignore the whole thing? Should I join in and let them haul me on board and slice off my blubber? Should I go on the rampage like Moby Dick and smash their boat to pieces? Or maybe just swim away with the rest of my pod?

The whaling boat was about ten metres away, and they were all straining at the imaginary oars while Fedallah got ready to hurl another harpoon at me, when my dilemma was solved by, of all people, Tamara Bello. She strolled up, looking like a species that had evolved far beyond the jabbering apes around her, took out a rather large imaginary pair of scissors, and cut the invisible rope attached to the harpoon.

I suppose the boat crew should have fallen backwards once the rope had been cut, but they weren't *that* good. Instead, they all just tutted and moaned and went off to do other stuff, not even bothering to step over the wooden walls of their boat or swim to shore, which you'd have thought was the least they could do. But then again, you'd need a will of iron to stand up to Tamara Bello . . .

And now she turned to me, hands on hips.

'You should learn to stick up for yourself,' she said, and then walked slowly away across the waves.

'I think she likes you,' said Renfrew, who then dodged away before I had the chance to kick him in the nuts.

More food-related misery tonight. My dad does his best to keep up with Mum's healthier eating programme, but it doesn't really work as his heart isn't in it. It's a bit like one of those really boring teachers who wears a novelty tie with Snoopy or Donald Duck or a pirate skull-and-crossbones on it to try and prove how 'crazy' he is. So, for tea tonight we had vegetarian sausages and sweet potato chips. The vegetarian sausages were the kind that have actual vegetables in them so you occasionally come across a complete pea or a hunk of carrot, which is the last thing you want to find in a sausage (imagine eating a pea and finding a whole little sausage in the middle of it – you'd be a bit concerned, wouldn't you?). And I can't even imagine what the sausagey stuff in between the vegetables is. Some mixture of soil and dog hair? Asbestos? We'll never know.

But it was the chips that I really objected to. 'Sweet' potato is one of the biggest lies in the history of the world. Some genius advertising guy must have thought that one up. I bet they were originally called 'not-very-nice-orange-potatoes'. Not even being turned into a chip – normally the greatest thing that can happen to a member of the potato family – can save the not-very-nice-orange-potato. For a start, they're orange. Who wants an orange chip? I'll answer that – NOBODY wants an orange chip. And one of the main jobs of a chip is to be crunchy on the outside. These not-very-nice-orange-chips were not in the least crunchy on the outside. They were as crunchy on the outside as a baby's bum cheek. The other major job of the chip is to be fluffy on the inside. These not-very-nice-orange-chips were all hard and crunchy on the inside. This meant that the eternal beauty of the chip – all that is great and noble about it – had been turned completely inside out. Sacrilege!

Well, I'd said about half of this, actually being quite funny about it – or so I thought – when I saw my dad's face. It had a look of total defeat on it. It reminded me of something. It was the way I felt on the inside last term when things had been at their lowest ebb, and I had no friends and all the world was against me.

So I said, 'Actually, Dad, this is pretty good.' And then I ate everything on my plate and asked for seconds.

DONUT COUNT:

Well, I had to get the taste of orange chips out of my mouth, didn't I?

Wednesday 17 January

Bad dreams in the night. I was being chased
through a forest of giant donut trees (that wasn't
the bad part – my best dreams usually involve
giant donut trees). I couldn't see what was
chasing me, but I heard its thunderous tread
and felt its breath hot on my neck. Somehow I
managed to climb a tree, out of range of those
chomping jaws. But the thing prowled around the
tree, waiting for me to fall into its gaping maw.

Actually, the dream slightly improved from

there on in, as I kept myself alive by eating the donuts on the donut tree. When I woke up I'd eaten half my pillow.

But I couldn't go on like this.

I was running out of pillows.

So, at break time, I shook hands with my friends, saying what I thought might be my final farewells, and went up to Ludmilla. She was sitting by herself on a concrete bench. She didn't seem to have many friends. Actually, she didn't seem to have *any* friends. She was concentrating hard on eating a Scotch egg.* She looked like an

---

* In case you don't know, a 'Scotch egg' is not the way in which the Scottish race reproduces itself (they give birth to live young, like the rest of us), but a savoury delicacy made from a hard-boiled egg wrapped in sausage meat and finally coated in breadcrumbs. They're actually quite nice, although they lie heavy as cannonballs in your stomach, and take about a month to digest.

ogre or troll, crunching on the skulls of innocent humans she'd captured in the forest.

'Ludmilla,' I said, and she looked up at me.

I'd been planning to say something like, *You seem to have got the idea that we're a couple. But we're not. The message on the banana wasn't for you, it was to the banana. I wouldn't go out with you if you were the last skull-crunching troll maiden on earth, so please stop persecuting me with bananas and chips.*

But then she looked up at me from her Scotch egg, and in that look there was so much . . . I don't know, hope and longing, that I just couldn't be mean to her. I thought about the terrible time I'd had during the first term, and how lonely it was possible to feel.

So I sat down next to her.

'Thanks for the banana,' I said. 'But I sort

of wish you hadn't written on it in your own blood.'

Ludmilla made a puzzled sound, a bit like a reasonably friendly gorilla who's found something that may or may not be edible on the forest floor.

She reached into her clothing and I thought she was going to pull out another bag of chips. But all that emerged in her big hand was a ballpoint pen. A *red* ballpoint pen.

'Oh, I see,' I said, rather embarrassed.

Ludmilla then offered me a bite of her Scotch egg.

'No thanks,' I said. 'I'm on a diet. You know. Healthy stuff only for me.'

Then I remembered that I did, in fact, have a donut in my pocket. I took it out and broke it in half and gave one of the halves to

Ludmilla. I didn't mind sharing the donut as it had raspberry-flavoured icing, which is only my ninth favourite flavour. She bit into it, even though she still had quite a lot of Scotch egg in her mouth. From then on she alternated bites between the donut and the Scotch egg. That seemed a waste of a perfectly good half-donut to me, but if there's one thing I've learned in life it's that people like different things and there's no point trying to argue about it, even if they are TOTALLY WRONG.

After a while I said, 'I don't really want a girlfriend, Ludmilla.'

Ludmilla stopped chewing for a couple of seconds. I suppose it was her way of showing extreme emotion.

'Maybe when I'm a bit older . . .' I paused. 'The thing is, I don't really know what to do with girls or how to talk to them. Except my sisters, and I mainly communicate with them by calling them names and throwing stuff at them.'

'*Pfumpf*,' she said, which was fair enough.

'So I think that we should just be friends. What do you think?'

'Banana,' she said, holding out her hand.

'What?'

'Banana!'

'Oh, yes.'

I took the banana she'd given me out of my pocket, and handed it back to her.

Strangely, as I walked away, I saw the FHK looking over at Ludmilla. He was smirking a smirk, although it wasn't quite his usual smirk. It was a bit less smirky than the normal smirk. No doubt he was enjoying my romantic difficulties.

'How was it?' asked Renfrew when I returned to the safety of my own lines.

'Not too bad. She's all right, actually, Ludmilla.'

'Are you still married to her?'

'Nah. But the divorce is, er, amicable. I get custody of the donuts and she gets the Scotch eggs, although I'm allowed to see them at weekends.'

DONUT COUNT:

I've decided to draw a line under the earlier mishap and start again.

Thursday 18 January

There has been a second pooping episode. Again, I found myself not very far from the scene of the crime. It was PE with the insane Mr Fricker, who lost both his hands in some kind of military incident before he became a teacher. We spend quite a lot of our time speculating about how this might have occurred. The latest theory is that his hands were chewed off by a starving camel.

We're doing rugby this term, which is slightly

better than cross-country running, and much, much worse than, say, eating a pizza. Mr Fricker usually joins in, doing really painful, crunching tackles on the kids he doesn't like, e.g. me. He has some special extra large rugby hands which he uses to catch the ball and shove you out of the way.

Doing PE is no fun, but there is one thing that's worse. Forgetting your PE kit is the absolute vilest sin in the Fricker universe. Forget your kit and he'll invent some terrible task for you to perform while the rest of the class run around on the sports field. Rumour has it that he once made a kid lick the wooden floor of the gym clean. Someone else told me that he drinks out of a cup made from the skull of a boy who forgot his kit two weeks running.

I was sure I'd packed my PE kit earlier that

morning, but when I looked in my bag in the changing rooms: zilch.

'You're doomed,' said Spam.

I went and stood in front of Mr Fricker. He was unscrewing his normal hand and screwing on his rugby hand. What looked like human hair was trapped under the fake nail.

'What is it, Millicent?'

'It's Milligan, sir.'

'I know who you are. I was being sarcastic. Millicent is a girl's name. I was suggesting that you are like a girl. A fat girl. Got that?'

'Yes, sir.'

'So, what do you want?'

'It's my kit, sir. I've——'

'Don't bother even finishing that sentence, Millicent.'

'Sorry, sir.'

Fricker screwed in the second giant rugby hand. It made a *skreek-skreek-skreek* noise as he rotated it. I think he did this as what is known as a Displacement Activity. This is when you do one thing even though you'd rather be doing another. The thing he'd rather be doing was unscrewing my head.

'I want you over in that corner, standing on one leg. I'm going to send a boy over every ten minutes. If he reports back that you are not standing on one leg, then I AM GOING TO COME BACK HERE AND TEAR THE LEG OFF AT THE SOCKET AND BEAT YOUR BRAINS OUT WITH IT. Got that?'

I went and stood on one leg in the corner of the gym, as indicated by the psychopath, and thanked my lucky stars that he was in a good mood.

The strange thing is that it turns out I'm actually quite good at standing on one leg. It was a double lesson, so that meant an hour and a half. Every ten minutes I changed legs. I did a bit of hopping to keep the circulation going. Only fell over twice. All in all, as an activity, it ranked midway between eating a pizza and getting attacked by Mr Fricker on the rugby pitch.

Anyway, the hour and a half passed. First the girls came in from netball. Ludmilla glanced over at me and raised her hand, as if she was about to give me one of her little waves. But she stopped halfway through, lifted her chin bravely and went on. The tight leotard and short yellow skirt weren't very flattering, but I still felt a pang of affection for the human girl inside the troll.

Then the boys came in from rugby. They were drenched by the rain and coated in mud,

and had the eyes of people who had seen
Terrible, Terrible Things. It was possible that
Mr Fricker's shorty shorts had rucked up his
horrific bumcrack again. I said a little prayer to
whichever deity it was that had made me forget
my PE kit. At the doorway, the battered war
veterans turned left and filed into the changing
rooms.

Seconds later, they ran out again. Their faces
were all twisted up – some with disgust, some
with laughter.

Mr Fricker appeared, carrying the rugby
ball and adjusting his shorts. The boys swarmed
around him. He looked puzzled, then furious,
then blank. His blank look was his most scary. It
meant he had gone beyond rage and into hatred.

I stayed in the corner on one leg.

Mr Fricker stomped off to his private office,

which was just a bit of the gym with a curtain round it. It was where he kept the special attachments for his arms – the ping-pong bat, the hockey stick, the car vacuum cleaner, the cake slice, the frying pan. When he sprang out a minute later, a large pair of metal tongs protruded from his left wrist socket. From his right was a good old-fashioned pirate's hook, on which hung a clear plastic bag. He stalked over to the changing rooms.

I should probably have stayed where I was, but I just couldn't stop myself from following. Nor could most of the other boys. Or the girls, including Miss Gunasekara – Mr Fricker's second in command – who was as nice as he was horrid.

And so we saw Mr Fricker approach the large greeny-brown poo, right in the middle of the changing-room floor. Saw him kneel down

before it like a Masai warrior tracking a lion.
Saw him grasp it firmly in the tongs and transfer
it to the plastic bag.

Behind us, there was a groan followed by a thud. Someone had fainted.*

Fricker turned and glared at us. He held up the bag with its gruesome contents showing through the clear plastic. 'Evidence!' he said.

His eye seemed to seek me out in the crowd.

Or maybe I was just being paranoid. Told Mum and Dad about the two poo incidents at dinner. Dad seemed quite interested, but Mum said it wasn't a fit subject for the dining table.

* This turned out to be Ludmilla, who had an unexpectedly delicate constitution. She had to spend the rest of the day in the sick bay. The sick bay is a grim and terrible room where you get sent if you are sick. All it contains is a sort of bed to lie down on and a bucket of sand to soak up the vomit if you puke. As the room smells of vomit most of the time, there's always a very good chance you will puke, as nothing makes you puke like the smell of puke. I think this is officially called a vicious circle. Of puke.

Ruby said that boys were disgusting, so I pointed out that for all we knew it could be a girl. She was too stupid to reply that the evidence actually suggested quite strongly that it was a boy, as the poos were in the boys' toilet and the boys' changing room. It's a sad state of affairs when you have to point out the flaws in your own logic.

As soon as the subject came up, Ella put her fingers in her ears and made cat noises.

No sign of Crow. Reckon he's been staked.

DONUT COUNT:

Friday 19 January

Nothing much happened at school today, which
was a relief after recent events. About the most
interesting thing was when Spam said, more or
less out of the blue:

'I heard that every time you do a fake burp
you lose an hour of your life.'

It took a while for that to sink in. I mean, the
stupidity of it.

'What the heck do you mean by a fake burp?'
I said. 'Do you mean when you deliberately

swallow air to make yourself burp, or do you mean when you haven't really burped at all, but just made a burp-like sound to try to impress people?'

'Well, I—'

'And how come it's exactly an hour? How would your body know? Is it, like, keeping count?'

'It's—'

'And how does anyone know that this is true? Have scientists captured some kids and strapped them to a burp-monitoring apparatus and kept them imprisoned in a lab all their lives until they die? 'Cos, basically, how else would you measure it?'

'I'm just—'

'And even if they did that, how would they know when you were supposed to die – you know, if you hadn't done any fake burps?'

'Easy, tiger,' said Renfrew, putting a restraining hand on my shoulder.

'Sorry,' I said. I'd been too hard on Spam, who was a gentle soul.

I blame the poo. It had put me on edge.

Mum took the girls out to see a movie tonight –
the sort of appalling load of old rubbish
where ladies go on about their shoes, hair,
feelings, etc. etc. etc., and then have to decide
whether to go out with the nice geeky bloke
or the cool handsome one, and they choose the
cool one – only to find out that he's nasty, and
he snogs their best friend, and then they end up
with the geeky one, who turns out to be quite
cool and really good-looking when he takes his
glasses off.

Obviously, I'd rather scoop out my eyeballs with a stale donut than go and see one of those films. So me and Dad spent the night watching *The Great Escape* for the eighteenth time and eating pizza. This was allowed because the pizza was a vegetarian one, but for once the vegetableness of it didn't ruin the pizzariness of it.

Despite the pizza and the movie, my dad still seemed a bit down in the dumps. I felt I should try to talk to him about . . . *things*. The trouble is, I don't really have the vocabulary for it. Maybe if I'd gone to the rubbish girlie movie with Mum and Ruby and Ella I could have picked up some tips.

So I had to take a plunge into the Unknown.

'You all right, Dad?'

'What? Oh, yeah.'

There was a pause for about ten minutes. We were at the part where Steve McQueen is bouncing the ball against the wall of the cooler.*

'Do you want the rest of your pizza, Dad?'

'Help yourself.'

---

* If you don't know what I'm talking about, then you should just watch *The Great Escape*, because it's the third most brilliant film in the history of the world.

Some more time went by. Steve McQueen tried to jump his motorbike over the fence and into Switzerland.

'Are you sure you're OK, Dad? It's just you seem a bit, er, not OK.'

My dad took a sip of his beer and I took a sip of my diet cola.

Then Dad did something unheard of. He paused the movie.

'The thing is, son, when you're an adult, sometimes you look around and you think, is that it? Have I already had all the good things and, from now on, is it only this? Because I didn't actually have that many good things, and it doesn't seem fair.'

I didn't really know what to say to that. And then, as if by magic, I sort of *did* know what to say next.

'Sometimes, Dad, when I get a box of donuts, I eat them without really paying attention to them. So I sort of waste them. All I get is the calories and the fat and the sugar, but not the fun. And then I look down and the donuts are all gone. And that's pretty depressing. But then it hits me: if I want to, tomorrow I can just go out and get some more donuts. Because there are still, you know, donuts out there, just waiting for you.'

My dad nodded and hit the 'play' button. And then, about five minutes later, he started to laugh and he threw a nibbled quadrant of pizza crust at me, and then I laughed too, and pretty soon we were laughing so hard we were spraying out pizza crumbs and cola and beer.

We were still laughing when the girls came in. They all had black lines on their cheeks from where their eye make-up stuff had run because of all the crying they'd been doing in their soppy film. So I reckoned that, in this particular war between boys and girls, we'd won 10–0.

DONUT COUNT:

All that talk of donuts had given me a craving for the real thing but a) I didn't have any, and b) I was quite full of pizza, and c) I had a funny feeling that something was coming – something that might need to be confronted with a stomach full of donut, so I'd better save up my allowance.

SATURDAY 20 JANUARY/
SUNDAY 21 JANUARY

Like I said, I'd known it was coming for a while,
but some ancient instinct for self-preservation
kept it from the forefront of my mind. 'It' was
Doc Morlock, the nutritionist who'd made my
life hell last term by banning donuts (or trying
to) and generally being mean – not to mention
her possession of a mouth like a cat's bum and a
vulture neck and scaly claws instead of hands.

Her main thing was poo. Yep, she was a world

expert. She could tell from your poo exactly what was wrong with you and what you should do to put it right – e.g. stop eating donuts, or do more exercise or whatever. Well, the thing is, she'd been given her own TV series on a rubbish satellite channel. It was called *Whose Poohs*.* On *Whose Poohs*, various minor celebrities would come on with samples of their poo, and Doc Morlock would have to work out which poo belonged to which celebrity.

It was definitely the most useless programme in the history of broadcasting.

And we had tickets to be in the studio audience.

We had tickets partly because I was Doc

* I think that they put the 'h' on to make it less rude, like it was just Winnie-the-Pooh they were talking about, rather than what comes out of your bottom.

Morlock's favourite ex-patient, as she had 'saved' me from my donut addiction. Or so she thought. I'd played a rather brilliant trick on her by substituting some healthy, vegetable-rich poo produced by a grumpy chimp called Samson for my own sugary, donut-flavoured poo. We were also going because my mum and Doc Morlock were now friends, which is a bit like the Nazi–Soviet Pact of 1939 that we did in history, except that my mum isn't really as evil as Hitler or Stalin, even if Doc Morlock is. Anyway, the pact meant that my mum could get as many tickets as she wanted, which isn't really surprising considering how terrible the show was.

So there we all were: me, Mum, Dad, Ruby. Ella said that she was too sick to come, which was both a massive, obvious lie and also the complete and utter truth, as she is, actually, sick.

(I mean the kind of sick that you say with a groan, as in 'You're sick, man,' and not the sick that means quite cool, as in 'That's a sick game.' Or, for that matter, the kind of sick that means you're dying of bubonic plague, or your finger's just dropped off because you've got leprosy.)

We had to be in our seats half an hour before the recording started, which was pretty boring. Then we had a guy who came on and told us some jokes that were so lame not even a schoolteacher would have bothered with them. His job, my dad told me, was to get us warmed up so we all sounded like we were enjoying ourselves when the actual programme started.

I suppose it was kind of interesting seeing how programmes got made. There were lots of people running around wearing headphones and carrying clipboards. There were lights, and there were microphones, and there were video monitors. There were just two cameras, which even I knew was a bit cheap and rubbish.

And then a sad-looking man did a sort of countdown with his fingers and we all had to clap.

Then Doc Morlock came out with a terrifying smile contorting her narrow lips. Despite the fact that she was all glammed up, in a posh frock and make-up as thick as school rice pudding, she looked more than ever like the Grand High Witch.

'And I know you'll all be as excited as I am when I welcome my guests today,' she said.

Then a man who'd once come third on *Big Brother* came out, followed by a woman who'd once snogged someone famous, and finally by an actor who'd been a heartthrob back in the

1970s, but who couldn't smile because he'd had so many facelifts his belly button was now where his mouth had once been. Where his mouth was, I didn't like to think . . .

Mum and Ruby both seemed to be enjoying themselves. I glanced over at Dad, and at the same moment he looked at me. A rare moment of understanding passed between us. We'd both stared into the Pit, and seen the demons and monsters and devils writhing there.

I can hardly bring myself to recount what happened next. Basically, the three 'celebrities' had given Doc Morlock their 'samples' earlier on. Then she talked about them, pointing out the good and bad sides of their poos. It was a bit like Goldilocks and the Three Bears. One was too hard, one was too soft, and one was just right.

Doc Morlock didn't stop at analysing the diets that had resulted in the three poos. She described one as being 'a typical Aquarius stool'. So it seemed that even poos had star signs. And she thought that one of the poos (the very hard one that looked like a burned cocktail sausage) was clearly indicative of a recent bereavement, or possibly divorce. I started thinking about poos getting married. I sort of hoped that they got married to other poos, or else someone was going to be very unhappy on their wedding night.

Anyway, the climax came, and Doc Morlock wrote down which poo belonged to which celebrity and put it in a sealed envelope. Then the studio audience got to vote as well, using the little buttons on the arms of our chairs. Mum and Ruby got all excited about it and discussed their choice as if it was the most important thing since the first humans climbed out of the trees. Dad, I noticed, used his voting finger to pick his nose. I decided to register my disapproval by randomly pressing buttons, thereby hoping to bring the system crashing down.

It didn't work.

The divorced poo belonged to the old actor. The sloppy one belonged to the girl who'd kissed someone famous, and the just right one belonged to the *Big Brother* guy. He was given a cheque for a thousand pounds to donate to his favourite charity, which he said was dedicated to giving sustainably produced organic bobble hats to mad people in Ecuador.

Doc Morlock got all the poos right, but I expect it was rigged. One person from the studio audience who'd got all three right was randomly selected by computer and won a prize, which turned out to be the three celebrity poos.

When we got home, Dad put the lights on in the living room, and suddenly we saw a tangle of spindly black-clad arms and legs springing apart. It was Ella and Crow. They'd definitely been snogging.

It was the most disgusting thing I'd seen all night. Including the poos.

I told my friend Jim all about it today (it's Sunday). Jim doesn't go to my school, so I only ever see him at weekends. He didn't believe a word of it. He said he knew that there was a lot of poo on the telly, but not real-life poo. So that's when I showed him the three samples of celebrity poo.

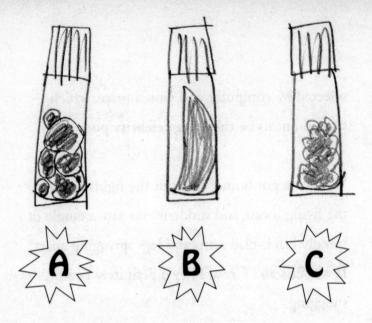

Yep, *I* was the lucky winner.

DONUT COUNT:

You're not going to believe this, but in spite of the IMMENSE provocations of the evening I kept to my target. My enemies should quake before me. Truly I am a boy with a WILL OF STEEL!

Monday 22 January

Now they're calling him the Brown Phantom.
Yes, there has been another attack. The third.
This time it was left steaming in the middle
of the corridor during morning break. I was
alone in our form room, desperately trying to
finish the geography homework I'd forgotten
about. The thing about Hairy Braintree, our
geography teacher, is that he never actually reads
what you've done, but just gives you a mark
depending on how much you've written. So,

technically, you could write any old rubbish, as long as it filled up a few pages.

Hence: 'Ecuador's biggest import is ethically produced bobble hats for the insane . . .' etc. etc.

So it wasn't that *hard*, but it had to be done, and so I missed most of the excitement.

Spam told me later that *it* was discovered by Miss Bush, the school secretary, and she had to be given counselling so that it didn't haunt her dreams for ever, which can apparently happen. I imagined her dying years later in a nursing home somewhere, her last moments on earth completely ruined by the giant poo, looming up at her like a king cobra about to strike. Miss Bush wasn't very nice, but she didn't deserve *that*. Nobody deserved *that*. Except maybe Genghis Khan, Hitler, Stalin, Chairman Mao, Doc Morlock and my sisters.

By the way, I'm adopting a light-hearted approach to this as a way of hiding the extreme pain and anguish in my soul. I bet you're thinking, How could the Brown Phantom possibly cause pain and anguish to me? Wasn't it exactly the sort of thing that would, in fact, add large amounts of happiness to my days? Yes, ordinarily. People pooping around the school was funny. Very funny.

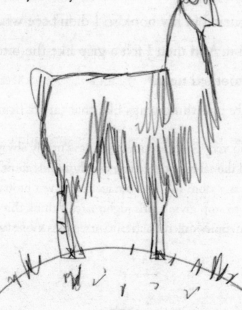

But the fun was about to stop.

I was lining up outside the geography room, adding a few final flourishes to my essay ('the Ecuadorians of Ecuador mainly eat llamas, except for Dalai llamas, which are held to be sacred throughout Latin America, Mongolia, Tibet, etc., and only eaten during religious ceremonies or on Good Friday, whichever comes first, when eating normal llamas is banned,' and so on).

I noticed a weird sort of silence, but I had my head buried in my book so I didn't see what had caused it. And then I felt a grip like the bite of a sabre-toothed tiger.*

Only one thing grips like that (apart from

---

* For no very good reason, this is now nearly always called the sabre-toothed cat, which sounds about as scary as a sabre-toothed sausage roll. It was probably done to stop giving girls nightmares. I think this is what is sometimes called Political Correctness Gone Mad.

sabre-toothed tigers, which aren't, of course, around any more to do any gripping, biting, etc.).

I looked up into the tight, mean, brittle face of Mr Whale, our Head of Year.

Apart from Mr Fricker, Mr Whale is the most feared teacher in the school. And at least Mr Fricker has the excuse of being insane to account for his behaviour. Mr Whale isn't mad at all. He is just really, *really* unkind.

Oh, and he's bald. Being bald is one of those things that changes its meaning depending on circumstances. If someone is especially nice, then them being bald becomes part of their niceness. My Uncle Geoff is a bit like that. He always gives us loads of money and is always saying nice but non-creepy things to me, such as, 'Hello, Dermot, here's ten pounds.' So *his* baldy head actually looks nice and friendly and generous.

But Mr Whale's is one of the evil baldy heads. If Mr Whale's baldy head was an animal it would be a box jellyfish, which is the deadliest creature in the oceans – except, of course, for Man, who is the deadliest creature pretty much everywhere, if you assume that the Alien and the Predator are just made up. And, frankly, if you don't assume that, you're a simpleton.

What's worse is that Mr Whale is the acting Deputy Head of the whole school while Mrs Vishnu is off having her baby.

'Follow me, boy,' said Mr Whale. He actually did that beckoning thing with his finger.

I looked at the guys in the line. Spam gulped. Renfrew looked like he was trying not to weep.

Corky had his eyes closed, probably in an attempt not to break wind, which was always a fatal mistake when Mr Whale was around. Even Tamara looked sympathetic.

Four and a half minutes later, I was facing Mr Whale as he arranged himself behind his office desk. It was the size of an aircraft carrier,

DEPUTY HEAD

which was probably meant to make Mr Whale
seem important, but actually made him look like
a midget.

Finally he was ready, and he fixed me with
his famous stare. His eyes were the colour of
dirty dishwater and he had no eyebrows. People
with no eyebrows always look like Evil Babies.
Especially when they are also baldy-heads. I
suppose it's probably the same the other way
round, and that Evil Babies always look like
baldy-headed teachers without eyebrows,
although I haven't made enough observations to
prove it scientifically.

'Do you know why you're here?' he said, after
a bit more staring.

I *was* actually pretty scared. It was probably
the Evil Baby thing. Evil Babies are scary,
and anyone who denies it is bluffing, or

has never been attacked by one.

'No, sir.'

'Guess.'

For some reason I thought it might be to do
with my geography homework, even though I
hadn't handed it in yet. I wasn't thinking straight.
It's hard to imagine it unless you've experienced
The Stare.

'The llamas, sir . . . ?'

'What? Llamas? Are you trying to be funny,
boy?'

'No, I—'

'Where exactly were you today between ten
forty-five and eleven fifteen?'

'Er, oh, I was in my form room, sir.'

'Doing what exactly?'

'Llamas . . . I mean my geography homework,
sir.'

'Who was there with you?'

'No one, sir. They were all at break.'

'How *very* convenient.'

'Not really, sir, I was—'

'And last Thursday – I understand that you were alone in the gym when the previous incident occurred?'

'Yes, sir. I was standing on one leg because I'd forgotten—'

'And before that? The original incident, the one on the floor of the boys' lavatory?'

'Then, sir? I was, er . . .'

Suddenly I could see where this was leading. And it wasn't to a good place. In fact, it was to one of the worst places you could imagine. Like being strapped right under the engine of a Saturn V rocket with the countdown to blast-off at 5–4–3–2 . . .

'Your form teacher, Mr Wells, says that you went to fetch your asthma inhaler, shortly before the first . . . the first . . . the initial *happening*. Is that correct?'

'Yes, sir, I—'

'Which means that yet again you had the opportunity.'

'But I—'

'Furthermore, I can find no mention in your school record of you having asthma . . . So if I were to call your father, Dermot, would he confirm, do you think, that you actually have asthma?'

Would he? Would my dad confirm that? I wasn't sure. My dad wasn't usually in a position to confirm anything other than the fact that yes, he was sitting on the toilet with his head in his hands.

But then perhaps Mr Whale was bluffing.

'Yes, sir. Give him a ring. The number's 77944395. He's usually at home during the day.'

Mr Whale's hand hovered over his phone. I looked nonchalant. I didn't feel nonchalant. I felt like that bit in *Alien* where the little dude bursts out of that guy's stomach.

Mr Whale's hand moved away from the phone.

'I'm prepared to accept for now, Dermot, the *possibility* that this is all just coincidence. The evidence is circumstantial. And there is nothing specific to indicate from your performance at school up until now that you're the kind of boy who would ... who would do *this* sort of thing. I believe that we're looking for a psychopath. Or at least a sociopath. But I will say this, Dermot. You are still under suspicion.

My eye is very much *on* you.'

And I felt it, like the burning red eye of the dark Lord Sauron himself.

DONUT COUNT:

I've decided to build some flexibility into my system to help me deal with these stressful times. So I'm aiming to average one a day, but with a tolerance factor of + or −1. Therefore, two still comes within my target range.

Tuesday 23 January

OK, we've hit a new low. Or high, given that it registered 11.8 on the Higgenthorpe Badness Scale. To put this into perspective, if I was a zebra, right now not only have I been ambushed by a pride of lions, and not only has the chief badass lioness got me by the throat, but the whole family has also come up and actually started eating me, without doing me the basic courtesy of waiting until I'm dead.

This is what happened.

I slept in. Only by ten minutes, but that set in motion a train of events that led to my downfall. Because I slept in, I was at the back of the queue for the bathroom. Which meant waiting twenty minutes for Ruby to pinkerize herself, and half an hour for Ella to transform herself from a normal human girl into the Queen of the Undead. Then Mum did her thing, which doesn't take that long because she's got very good at hiding what she really looks like with the aid of stuff she puts on her face. Then there was Dad, and I don't even want to think what he does in there, but he always comes out looking older and sadder than before.

By the time I'd finished brushing my teeth and peeling some of the dead skin from between my toes (yep, I've got athlete's foot without having to go to all the bother of being an actual athlete), I was already on the Road to Perdition, i.e. there was no way I was getting to school on time. So I began to take it easy, thinking that half an hour late gets you into exactly the same amount of trouble as ten minutes late.

So I had a leisurely breakfast of tea, toast, Weetabix, Shredded Wheat and pizza (I found a slice left over from the other night). I was careful not to write anything potentially embarrassing on my mid-morning snack banana – just giving it the classic shark makeover with an evil, grinning mouth and three vertical gill-slits.

'You should grow up,' said Ruby, looking at it like it was chewing-gum on the sole of her shoe. So, naturally, I attacked her with the banana, which was quite satisfying, although that took up even more time and meant that the banana was a bit bruised and battered.

Then I went to the bus stop, getting there just in time to see a bus trundling away. I ran to catch it at the traffic lights and gave the bus driver a pleading look, but he just made a rude gesture, roughly translated as: 'Get lost, fatty.'

Naturally I made a rude gesture back, roughly translated as: 'I may be a fatty, but when I grow up I'll probably get a decent job and have an OK life, whereas you are a bus driver, and a rubbish one at that, plus you stink, so you'll never get a decent girlfriend, etc. etc.'

Yes, you can do a lot with a gesture, if you put enough effort into it.

So I had to wait another twelve minutes for the next bus. But I didn't mind because usually when you miss the bus you can guarantee that it will be raining, but right now it wasn't.

Yay!

Anyway, by the time I got to school the half an hour late had turned into forty-five minutes. I expected to have to walk into the middle of double maths with Mr Kennilworth, who always looks like you've caught him out doing something embarrassing, even though he's actually too boring to be properly embarrassing. But I sensed straight away that there was something wrong. You can see into some of the classrooms, and they should have been full of bored-looking kids. But they were as empty as a six-box of donuts five minutes after I've opened it.

This could mean only one thing: an Emergency Special Assembly. If I was caught wandering around the school during an Emergency Special Assembly then I'd get massacred.

I hurried along to the hall, hoping to sneak in at the back. Before I reached it, I heard the muffled sounds of Mr Whale's insidious voice. I read somewhere that the best way to kill someone is to stab them with an icicle. Once the icicle has melted, there's no murder weapon, so the police can't get you. Mr Whale's voice is a bit like that icicle. Cold and deadly: killing you without leaving a trace.

There are three ways into the hall. The first is via the big sliding doors at the back. Then there are two smaller doors, one on each side, nearer the front. I decided to try the big back door, hoping that everyone would be facing the front, and that maybe Mr Whale would be too busy being sly and insidious to notice me.

I reached the hall and, to my relief, saw that there was a nice Dermot-sized gap in between the doors. I sneaked up and looked in. Mr Whale was on the stage with a couple of other teachers – Mr Fricker and Miss Choat, who, with her long neck and small head and big eyes and beaky mouth, looked as much like an ostrich as you could look whilst still being (more or less) human.

The hall was packed, and there were loads of other teachers standing at the sides.

'These events will not be tolerated,' I heard Mr Whale saying. Then he dropped a piece of paper, and bent down to pick it up. I took my chance – there were a couple of seats in the back row, and if I could just slip in and nab one I'd be safe.

I squeezed into the gap. My head was through. My chest was through. But that was it. My belly, swollen with my slightly-bigger-than-average breakfast, just wouldn't fit. And, worse – I couldn't get back out. I was stuck like a cork in a bottle.

And – could it have been my imagination? – the gap between the doors seemed to be getting smaller. I was being CRUSHED TO DEATH.

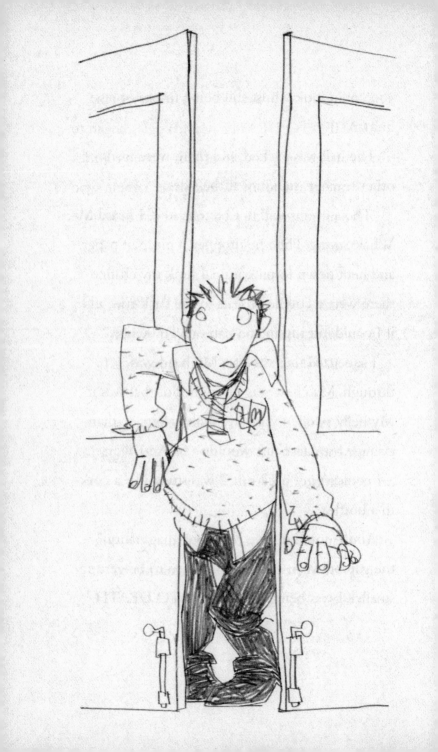

Few things make a boy panic more than being CRUSHED TO DEATH. My struggles began to attract attention. A couple of kids turned round. And some of the teachers. The more people who saw, the more noise there was. First grins. Then some laughter.

Mr Whale was standing again, after finding his notes. And now I'd caught his attention. That wasn't good. Plus there was the whole being CRUSHED TO DEATH thing that I had going on.

Then, relief.

Someone had slid the doors wide enough for me to fall through. And fall I did, right into the arms of my rescuer, who turned out to be none other than the Floppy-Haired Kid.

Miss Brotherton was the first teacher to reach me.

'Sit down and be quiet,' she hissed, not really distinguishing between me and the FHK.

'Thanks,' I said, when we were safely in the back row. In reply he gave me a little smile.

Mr Whale finished saying what he had to say. I still hadn't quite worked out what it was all about. I looked quizzically at the FHK.

'The Phantom,' he mouthed back silently.

'And now,' added Mr Whale, 'I'm going to pass you over to the headmaster, who will add some further words of his own.'

This statement produced a gasp from the assembled school kids. The Head, Mr Steele, is famously frail and feeble-minded. He only ever appears in public to announce the school sports results during the normal Friday assembly. He has literally never been seen at any other time or in any other place.

And now he was shuffling towards the microphone. Being forced to change the routine he'd kept to for the past twenty years had clearly further confused his mental state. Even from the back I could see that he didn't have any shoes on, and that one horny toenail had sliced its way through a dirty grey sock. He was dressed in what had probably once been a perfectly OK suit, woven from a mixture of asbestos, horsehair and belly-button fluff, but now it was in a pretty terrible state, with curious yellow and brown stains, as if the old headteacher had dribbled an egg-and-gravy sandwich down his front.

He reached the mic.

He stared with milky eyes around the hall.

He strolled away again, obviously convinced that he'd done whatever it was that he was supposed to do. Mr Whale firmly guided him back to the mic, and whispered urgently in his ear. Then he passed him the piece of paper he'd picked up off the floor. It was obviously a speech he'd written out for the Head.

Mr Steele began. The first few words were confident. For a moment, he seemed like a young man in his fifties and not the nonagenarian that he usually appeared.

'As you will no doubt have . . .'

But he could not sustain it. His eyes wandered from the notes prepared for him. He tried to find something else in the wide space of the hall to spur himself into action. And then, suddenly, he had left us for another time, another place, another universe.

'The Upper Sixth ice-hockey team has . . .'

Again Mr Whale approached and whispered. This time he looked a little angrier.

Mr Steele was dumbfounded. 'What, no ice hockey?' he said, his feeble voice caught and amplified by the mic. 'There is no ice? Or hockey? Oh. I see. I see.'

He focused on the paper again. 'Ah yes. The, ah, the dirty. The human dirt. This will not do. Really. Do, it will not.'

He looked over at Mr Whale, who nodded encouragement.

'And nor, if I may say so, will not this do. I repeat again, IT. NOT. DO. WILL.'

This brought a small cheer from the audience. The cheer perhaps over-stimulated Mr Steele.

'Well, thank you very much, and my con-gratulations to the girls' second eleven dwarf-throwers, who came a creditable nineteenth in the . . . in the . . . ah. Well, good luck and good night. The lights are going out all over Europe. Ask not what your country can do for you, but for whom the bell tolls. You can lead a horse to water, but a pencil must be led.'

Then Miss Choat came over on her backwards-bending ostrich legs, took his arm and guided him off the stage.

This meant that the stage belonged again to Mr Whale.

'Thank you, Headmaster,' he began, glancing at Mr Steele's receding figure. Then he turned the Evil Eye on us. 'Do not doubt that we will catch the person who is doing this. And when we've caught him – or her, if a her it be – then the full might of the law will be brought to bear.' He smashed his fist into his palm to add emphasis. 'And until we find the culprit, all morning breaks will be spent in your form rooms.'

Groans and half-choked cries of 'No!' rose from the crowd. They were quelled by another glare.

'Dismissed,' said Mr Whale, and that was it.

Normally, of course, me getting stuck in the giant hall doors would have created a sensation, but the Special Assembly devoted to the catching and smashing of the Phantom was such a unique and memorable event that my own little mishap seemed to be forgotten. However, I hadn't forgotten that the FHK had given me a hand when I needed it most. So I went and thanked him at lunch time.

'Forget it,' he said in his usual careless way, as if my thanks meant absolutely nothing to him. But it didn't change the fact that he'd helped me out, and might not be such a swine after all.

DONUT COUNT:

Still within the new revised target . . .

Wednesday 24 January

Things very tense at school today. Everyone on edge. The Phantom could be anyone. Could be anywhere. The atmosphere was as thick as one of Corky's fruitier farts.

The boredom of morning break spent trapped in the form room was somewhat alleviated by a game called Speedbum, invented by Renfrew. In Speedbum, what you do is distract someone, e.g. by knocking their pen on the floor or by telling them that their shoelaces are undone or by looking out of the window and exclaiming loudly that the alien invasion of Earth has begun. You then see how many times you can write the word 'bum' on their exercise book. Corky turned out to be the world record holder at Speedbum. He managed fifty-seven bums in the time it took Spam to go to the wastepaper bin and back. His Speedbum expertise has probably got something to do with his Tourette's syndrome, which makes him want to swear all the time, and a stutter that means he can never get it out. It's tragic, really. But also very funny. I suppose that's what they call a paradox.

Tamara Bello watched all this with a Queen Victoria face. So when she was searching for something in her bag, I wrote an absolutely tiny 'bum' on her book, so small you'd only be able to see it with a microscope. Still, that showed her.

On my other side, Ludmilla had
a different sort of look on her face.
It was more a 'let me join in' sort of
look. But I didn't want to encourage
her into thinking that the banana
message was true all along or anything
like that. And if I wrote 'bum' on her
book, she might think I was saying
that I thought she had a nice bum. Or
a rotten one. It was a lose-lose situation
if ever there was one. There's a time and
a place for writing 'bum' on someone's
exercise book, and this clearly wasn't it.

Crow was round at ours again tonight.
He actually said a few words in human
language, rather than just using his finger.
He's not that bad when you get to know

him. The funny thing is, he's got a weekend job selling ice cream. That in itself cheered me up after the recent traumas – just the thought of Crow in a white coat handing out choc-ices and 99s was enough to make me giggle. An ice-cream-selling Goth seemed pretty far-fetched. But then, as I said at the time, life is full of far-fetched things, such as Ella finding someone just as weird as her to go out with. Then I ran for it, to avoid getting jabbed in the eye by one of Crow's giant fingers, or vamped to death by Ella.

DONUT COUNT:

Thursday 25 January

Yesterday was like one of those days in a war when nothing much happens and you can hang out your washing on the barbed wire and play football in no-man's-land.

Well, today was different.

I was settling down at my desk for English with Miss Brotherton, contemplating a quick round of Speedbum, when two prefects came in. One was my old enemy, Ivan the Terrible. He was still limping from his mishap with the poo, but it looked like it had just been a sprain and not a break.

Pity.

I didn't know the name of the other prefect, but he always followed Ivan around, the way a smell of egg follows a fart. He had a zit on the side of his nose that was actually bigger than the nose itself, so it looked like the spot had a nose rather than the other way round. Ivan was no genius, but the spotty prefect was the kind of kid who'd stick his finger up his bum and act surprised when it didn't smell of flowers.

'We've come for Milligan. Mr Whale wants him,' said Ivan, not showing very much respect for Miss Brotherton. That was quite risky. Miss Brotherton could be pretty fierce, in a big-nosed, woodpeckery kind of way. Which,

I admit, is not the fiercest kind of fierce, but it's
more fierce than being fierce in a rabbitty
way, for example. But today Miss Brotherton
wasn't even woodpecker-fierce. She looked
a bit sad. She was going out with Mr Wells, so
maybe they'd had an argument, or he'd decided
that her nose was just too big and her elbows
too sticky-outy, even if she did have quite
nice hair.

So she just waved me out of the room, like a
bored judge waving a condemned man off to the
gallows.

On the way to Whale's office, the two prefects
kept shoving me against the walls and tripping
me up and the usual prefect tricks.

'Bouncy bouncy,' sneered Ivan.

I really hate that kid.

Really.

Hate.

That.

Kid.

'Stepped in any poo lately?' I asked sweetly,
and got a last cuff round the head as my answer.

We reached Mr Whale's office.

'Wait here, Lardy,' said Ivan, and then the two

goons went off to find someone else to torment.

I could see through the frosted glass that there were several people in there. I'll admit that I was sweating. I guessed that this had to be about the Phantom. But as far as I was aware there hadn't been any more attacks.

The door opened and a face appeared. It wasn't a good face to see at that moment.

'Millicent, in,' said Crazy Fricker.

What awaited me in the room was pretty close to my dream team, if by 'dream team' you mean the group of people most likely to make me want to curl up in the corner and whimper.

Mr Whale was there, of course, looking more like an Evil Baby than ever. Then there was Mr Fricker, who I now saw was wearing his sensible hands rather

than any special attachments. And, completing

the unholy trinity, DOC MORLOCK!!!

Actually, there was one friendlier face in there: Mr Wells. Mr Wells was OK. He said 'well' too much, but there are worse faults than that, e.g. looking like an Evil Baby, or enjoying torturing kids on the rugby field, or spending your life looking at poo and telling people to stop eating donuts.

I also noticed that there was a deeply revolting smell in the room, despite the fact that the window was open. And a big fat bluebottle was buzzing around, like a cherry on the cake of irritation.

Mr Whale started talking, although I missed the first part because the horror of all this had rendered me temporarily deaf.

'. . . international expert . . . consultant with the Metropolitan Police Forensic Department . . . brought in to solve this dastardly . . .'

I shook my head and tried to get my brain
into gear.

'It is not public knowledge yet,' continued
Mr Whale, 'but there was another incident.
It occurred yesterday. During assembly. The
assembly into which *you* were observed sneaking
significantly late.'

'It was my sisters, sir . . . in the bathroom . . .
and the bus . . . the driver . . .'

My excuses petered out, defeated by the looks
of disgust, boredom, etc. etc. on the faces before me.

'It was here. In my office. The inner sanctum.
There.'

Whale pointed to his wastepaper bin.

It sank in.

The Brown Phantom had
dumped in the acting Deputy
Headmaster's wastepaper bin.

In another situation I'd have been rolling around on the floor. But I realized that I was deep in the poo, just like the poo was deep in the bin.

'But how do you know it was done during assembly?'

'The . . . *object* was not discovered until this morning. It had been covered with a sheet of paper. I called in Doctor Morlock, who is an old friend, as well as someone who has helped me with . . . well, that's not relevant. She was able to give an approximate time of . . . *argh*—'

'Between nine-seventeen and ten-oh-six yesterday morning,' cut in Doc Morlock.

'And I also asked her to use her professional expertise to tell me if there were any other unusual or distinguishing features of the . . . evidence.'

'Stool, Mr Whale,' said Doc Morlock. 'I like to call a stool a stool.'

'Fine. Stool.'

'And'– for the first time the nutritionist looked directly at me, and her mouth was basically the most like a cat's bum that it has ever been, and it had always been a lot like a cat's bum – 'I can confirm that it was a very unusual stool.'

'How unusual, Doctor Morlock?'

Something about the way Mr Whale asked this made me think that it was prearranged.

'I have only ever seen one human stool like this before.'

'And when was that, Doctor Morlock?'

'It was at the end of last year.'

'And who did the, ah, *stool* belong to?'

She turned to me again, giving me the full cat's bum.

'It belonged to this boy here. Dermot. Dermot Milligan.'

Even though I guess they all knew what she was going to say, there was still a gasp from the other teachers.

'Well, how can you be sure, Doctor Morlock?' said Mr Wells, who was trying to stick up for me. 'Isn't one, *you know* . . . just like another, *you know* . . . ?'

'It certainly is not,' said the offended nutritionist. 'I can distinguish between forty-seven different types and sub-types. But this particular stool had large quantities of partially digested banana skin in it, and, as I have said, I have only ever seen that in one human stool sample: Dermot Milligan's.'

Mr Wells's face changed. He was remembering my stunt with the banana skin. Suddenly a much sterner character replaced the friendly Mr Wells.

'Well, I see,' he said.

'I can explain,' I said desperately.

I *could* explain it. Last year, Doc Morlock was watching my poo like a hawk to check to see if I was eating any of the banned donuts. If I was, then I was going to be sent to Camp Fatso. My choice was simple: stop eating donuts or get my hands on some 100% guaranteed prime quality, donut-free poo. I came by a dollop belonging to a bad-tempered chimp called Samson, which I passed off as my own.

Samson was too stupid to peel his bananas, which was why Doc Morlock now thought that any human poo with chunks of banana skin in it must be mine. So, to explain why the poo couldn't be mine would involve admitting that I was a HUGE LIAR. And it would be

Camp Fatso, here I come.

And anyway, who would believe me?

'We're waiting,' said Mr Whale.

'I've been framed. The whole thing's a set-up.'

Mocking laughter.

'And who would want to frame a schoolboy?'

'I've got . . . enemies.'

Mr Whale shook his head impatiently. 'I think we've heard enough of this, boy. It's time to confess. If you admit what you've done there may be a way to avoid expelling you, although of course you will need some psychiatric assessment, because clearly whoever has done this is mentally deranged.'

'Look, I absolutely promise that it wasn't me . . . That's not my . . . Really, it isn't.'

'Well, the evidence seems to be clear, Dermot,' said Mr Wells, looking as if I'd betrayed him.

'There is one sure way of finding out if this boy is lying.'

These were the first words uttered by Mr Fricker since I'd come in.

Mr Whale looked at him. 'Oh, and what's that?'

'Lie detector.'

'And you have one of those?'

'Oh yes, left over from my old SAS days, when I was one of the chief interrogators.'

'But I thought you were in the Catering Corps?'

'Well, yes, but we had squaddies pilfering rations all the time. It was my job to track them down and make them confess.'

'Well, I'm sorry,' said Mr Wells, 'but I can't allow one of my students to undergo that sort of interrogation. It's against the Human Rights Act. I guess.'

Mr Wells was probably trying to help me again, but a lie detector was exactly what I wanted, because for once I was telling the truth.

'I'll take it!' I said. 'Then you'll all believe me. Will you at least wait until then before you tell my parents?'

Mr Whale looked around at the others in the room. Then he nodded curtly.

'When can this be done, Mr Fricker?'

'Tomorrow lunch time. I'll bring in my apparatus in the morning, but it takes a while to calibrate.'

'Let's hope for your sake, Dermot, that the results are positive.'

'Negative,' said Fricker. 'Positive would mean he was lying.'

Mr Whale did not like to be contradicted.

'Whatever,' he snapped, and then we were all dismissed.

I briefly thought about fessing up to Mum and Dad so I could at least get my side of the story in first. But I couldn't face it. They had troubles of their own. My mum's company were getting rid of loads of people, and my dad only earned enough from his job to keep him in toilet paper. I had to beat this thing on my own.

DONUT COUNT:

Friday 26 January

I was in a terrible state this morning, waiting for the lie-detector test. It wasn't helped by the fact that I could sense that people were staring at me and whispering behind my back. I was used to people laughing at me, but this was different. Suddenly I wasn't a figure of fun any more. I was . . .

Evil.

Sorta.

Coooooooooool!

Well, no not really cool. Or cooooooooool! Because, after all, it involved poo, which is the opposite of cool.

When he took the morning register, Mr Wells said 'Milligan' in a funny way, which seemed to shout out, 'Milligan, also known as the Brown Phantom'.

Tamara Bello inched her desk as far away from me as it would go. And Ludmilla didn't even look at me. So there were a couple of up-sides! I'm kidding. It was all pretty bleak.

At morning break, Renfrew took me to one side.

'Everyone's saying it's you, you know.'

'The Brown Phantom, you mean?'

'Yep.'

'I know.'

'And are you?'

'Do you really have to ask me?'

'Well, it does look bad . . .'

'Et tu, Renfrew.'*

'I just had to ask.'

'Fine.'

I went to the gym at lunch. The guys came
with me as far as the door, but left me there.
Some things a boy has to do on his own, such as
having a wee and getting his fingernails pulled
out by Mr Fricker.

The man himself was waiting for me outside

---

* 'Et tu, Brute' were Julius Caesar's last words, spoken
to his best mate Brutus, when Brutus stabbed
him in the guts. It probably means something like:
'Get stuffed, Brutus, you dirty scumbag.' Actually,
his last words are more likely to have been,
'*Aaaaaaarrrrrgggggghhhhhh . . .*'

174

his office. He hadn't chosen which set of hands to wear yet, and he beckoned me with a bare stump.

Inside there was a table and two chairs. On the table stood a large box, with dials on the front and wires coming out of the back. On top of it there was a red light and a green light.

There was also a rack on the wall with Fricker's special hands. He selected a pair encased in tight-fitting leather gloves. These were his much-feared Interrogation Hands. As soon as he had them screwed in, he seemed to change. Gone was the hot-tempered shouty psychopath. In its place was something colder and more clinical and, in a way, even scarier.

'Sit down, Millicent,' he said. 'I'm just going

to attach these wires to your fingers. Nothing to worry about – they simply record temperature and moisture levels and electrical activity.' He taped wires to both my forefingers. He was surprisingly adept with his gloved hands. 'There, comfortable?'

'Not really, sir.'

'Good. I'm going to begin by asking you some simple questions. Answer as truthfully as you can.'

'OK.'

'Tell me your name.'

'Dermot Francis Milligan.'

The green light came on. Fricker checked the dials on his machine. He made a little grunting noise.

'How old are you?'

'I'm twelve years old.'

Another green light. Another check, another
grunt.

'What do you think of bananas?'

'I like them.'

After a brief pause, the red light came on.

Fricker raised an eyebrow. 'Really? I suggest you reconsider your answer.'

'OK, I love them.'

Green light.

'Excellent. Now tell me, where were you two Mondays ago at eleven-fifteen a.m. when the first outrage took place?'

I had to think fast. Did I own up about being in the toilets, or did I try to fool the machine?

Well, a wise man once said that you should only tell lies when you really have to, or when you are trying to stop girls from crying. This time I was going to use truth as my shield and honesty as my sword.

'I was in the school toilet.'

Green light.

'What were you doing there?'

'I was sitting in the cubicle.'

Green light.

'And?'

'That was it, sir. I heard someone come in and chuck something on the floor. When I got out of the cubicle, it was just there, on the floor.'

'The stool?'

'Yes, the poo.'

Mr Fricker stared at me, and then the green light went on.

For the next ten minutes Mr Fricker asked me about all the other incidents. I got green-lighted on everything. At the end he stood up, and spoke facing away from me.

'There's something you should know about me, Millicent.'

'Sir?'

'I am an implacable enemy. Get on the wrong side of me and—' He spun and slammed his leather-clad metal hand down on the table, karate-style, with a terrific crash. 'But if I'm your friend, then . . . well, let's just say that I can make your life easier. I think you're innocent, Millicent. But, frankly, that may not be enough to save you.'

'What do you mean, sir?'

'There's been a crime, and the top brass want a scapegoat. At the moment, that's you. I can try to keep them off your back for a while, but unless we're able to find the real criminal behind all this, then I'm afraid . . .' He seemed to be a bit lost for the appropriate words or gesture, so once more, with a mighty 'Ay-yah!' he karate-chopped the table.

'Were you really just in the Catering Corps, sir?' I asked him.

'It pays me to let them believe that, Millicent.'

'One more thing, sir,' I added. 'Your lie detector . . .'

'Yes?'

'It was just rubbish, wasn't it, sir? I mean, you just pressed a button to make the red or green light go on.'

'Get out of here, Millicent,' he said, but I thought I spotted a faint smile on his face as he said it.

DONUT COUNT:

Yeah, I know that's crashed through the new limit, but I thought I'd earned a small reward for writing such a massive entry in the Donut Diary.

Saturday 27 January/
Sunday 28 January

I called a full War Council on Saturday. All the
guys came round, plus Jim. We did it sitting on
the wall by the canal. We figured it was best
to be out of range of any listening devices.
However, my opponents seemed to be very well
equipped and financed, so there was a chance
the ducks might have been bugged. Corky
wanted to throw some stones at them to scare
them away, but I thought that was going a bit

far, as the chance of them really being bugged was about one in a billion, and the chance of us being fined for stoning ducks was much higher, so I said, 'Let he who hath not sinned cast the first stone,' which I remembered from church. Nobody cast any stones, although Jim did push me off the wall and kicked me a couple of times when I tried to climb back up.

Then we began. I summed up the recent events for those who were not fully abreast of the situation. When Jim had stopped laughing, I carried on:

ME: So, basically, my theory is that the Brown
    Phantom is just out to frame me.
SPAM: Cool. It's like we're in a movie.
ME: It's not in the least bit cool, Spam. I'm
    going to get expelled.

SPAM: Yeah, sorry, not cool.

JIM: But funny – you have to admit it's quite funny.

ME: You wouldn't think it was funny if it was you getting framed.

JIM: Yeah, but if it was me it really wouldn't be funny.

ME: How do you work that out?

JIM: No offence, Donut,* but it's because you're fat. That makes everything slightly funnier. It's not fair, I know, but I don't make the rules.

ME: Can we please stop talking about how fat I am, and get down to business?

* My school friends mainly call me Donut now, which I don't mind, and Jim has picked up the habit, even though it sounds a bit weird when he says it. Personally, I think school nicknames should stay in school, and home friends should think of different nicknames or just use your actual name, e.g. Dermot.

RENFREW: Donut's right. We should try and
find out who's behind this.

ME: Exactly – we have to unmask the Brown
Phantom.

JIM: How do you know he wears a mask? It'd
be a bit stupid, wearing a mask around school.
A teacher would just tell him to take it off
and then everyone would know who the
Brown Phantom was. You may as well just go
around with a sign saying 'Me, I'm the Brown
Phantom'.

ME: It was just a . . . Oh, never mind.

SPAM: We could be like detectives!

RENFREW: Bagsy I'm Sherlock Homes!

SPAM: You can be him. He's lame. I'm Batman.

RENFREW: Batman's not a detective, you
doofus.

ME: What is he, then?

RENFREW: He's a superhero.

SPAM: A *crimefighting* superhero, i.e. a detective.

RENFREW: My dad's got a Sherlock Holmes hat.

CORKY: (*Emits a short, sharp fart, indicating disapproval.*)

ME: Corky's right. This isn't helping me. I need to find out who the Brown Phantom is, and I need to find out fast. Any ideas?

JIM: Any thingamajig . . . *surveillance* footage?

RENFREW: Nah. All the security cameras at school are just dummies.

ME: How do you know?

RENFREW: My brother and a load of other Year Tens all mooned one of them at the end-of-year disco, and nothing happened.

CORKY: T–t–t–t–t—

ME: Exactly, Corky.

JIM: You should set a trap.

ME: How?

JIM: Well, as I see it, the Phantom has only ever
struck when you haven't got an alibi. That's
the weakness in your defence. But it's also
a weakness in the Phantom that you can
whaddya–call–it . . . *exploit*.

ME: I don't get it . . .

RENFREW: I see . . . it's a way we can control
the Phantom. He'll make his move when
you're on your own, without anyone to say
you didn't do it.

JIM: Yeah, exactly. Make sure he knows you're
alone, then he'll strike, and you'll be ready to
nab him.

ME: That's one thing that's really been bugging
me. How the heck does he know where I am?

I mean, like the first time, even I didn't know
I was going to the loo until I actually went.

SPAM: He must have followed you.

RENFREW: But how? No one else left our
classroom after you.

CORKY: Sp-sp-sp-sp—

ME: A spy, Corky? You mean there was a spy in
our class who must have informed on me?

SPAM: Could be.

RENFREW: How?

SPAM: Text would be the obvious way.

RENFREW: They'd have to be sly about it,
though. Mobiles being banned in school
and all.

ME: Right, we've made progress. We've got two
possible lines of investigation. We know the
Phantom has someone on the inside, someone
leaking information. And we know that he'll

strike again when I'm alone. The spy could lead us straight to the Phantom. And even if they don't, then we can trap him when he tries to trap me.

SPAM: I told you it was like a movie. And I've changed my mind. I'm going to be 007. Batman's for babies.

RENFREW: I'll stick with Sherlock Holmes. He's a classic, and the classics never go out of style. Plus, I've got the hat.

JIM: There's another thing. The Brown Phantom creep has somehow got hold of a load of old chimp poo, yeah?

ME: Yeah.

JIM: Well, that's another clue you've got – where do you get hold of chimp poo?

SPAM: The internet?

JIM: Think you can download it, do you?

SPAM: No, but . . .

JIM: Whoever it is has a reliable source of chimp doo-doo. Find the source, catch the Phantom.

ME: Excellent. Three lines of investigation. We have our work cut out, gentlemen.

That was yesterday. Today, I plotted and planned and texted.

And ate some donuts.

I also spent some time in the lavatory, groaning loudly and faking some rather horrible noises.

Why?

Go and look up 'suspense' in the dictionary.

By the way, Dad seems a bit more cheerful since our talk. I think maybe I should write a book in which I solve all the problems of the world using donuts. Global warming, the

Arab–Israeli conflict, runaway population growth, etc. etc., could all solved by the surgical application of donuts.

DONUT COUNT:

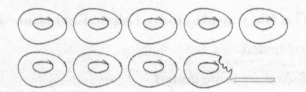

I know that seems excessive, but I brought extra supplies for the War Council, then forgot to hand them out. And then what was I supposed to do – throw them away?

Monday 29 January

The plan was desperate, but desperate times called for desperate measures by desperate kids in desperately large trousers. And those big trousers of mine needed to be filled to the brim with courage, because this was going to need more than I had ever called on before in the whole of my life. And it was quite possible that my reserves would dry up before the end, and my trousers prove to be empty.

It had also involved quite a lot of preparation.

At 11.30, in Mr Khan's chemistry lesson, I swallowed my pride, gritted my teeth and put up my hand.

'What is it, Dermot?'

'I need to go to the toilet, sir.'

'You know you're not permitted during lesson time. Just hold it in for another half an hour.'

'I can't sir. I've got terrible . . . terrible . . . diarrhoea.'

Appalled groans and sniggers from all around.

'I've got a note, sir, from my dad.'

And I did.

That was the reason behind all that moaning in the bog yesterday. Mum and Dad got quite worried about it. They even said that I could take the day off school. So I got extra brownie points for saying no, I was determined to go to school unless I was quite literally Killed to Death by my diarrhoea.

NOTE TO SELF: DON'T MENTION BROWNIE POINTS WHEN YOU'RE TALKING ABOUT DIARRHOEA – IT JUST SOUNDS REALLY YUCKY.

But they gave me a note in case I was caught out in lesson time. I handed it to Mr Khan. I could see him search his memory banks for a suitable joke. He came up with:

'OK, why do the Teletubbies all have to go to the toilet at the same time?'

No one answered. No one cared.

'Because they've only got one Tinky Winky!'

No laugh.

'So can I go, sir?'

Poor old Khan nodded, defeated again in his attempt to amuse the class.

I made my way to the bog – the same one I'd gone to when this whole nightmare had begun. I hid behind the door, and waited.

This was the plan: Spam was supposed to wait five minutes and then ask Mr Khan if he could go and check on me to make sure I was OK, as I looked so sick. So he'd be behind the Phantom and I'd be in front, and he'd be trapped like a rat in a . . . well, in a toilet.

The waiting part went well – I even got in some more practice at standing on one leg, just in case it was accepted as an event at the Olympics. With any luck it would be divided into weight categories, like boxing and weight-lifting, so I wouldn't be up against a load of skinny people who would find it easy to stand on one leg more or less for ever.

And then I heard the soft tread of someone approaching down the corridor. This was it. This was the moment I'd been waiting for. It would be like when Sam Gamgee finally gets his hands on Gollum in the third part of *The Lord of the Rings*. Then I remembered that Gollum actually beat Sam in their fight, as he employed Evil Girlie Tactics such as biting, crafty little blighter that he was. The Brown Phantom was definitely evil and might well be girlie, which considerably increased the chance of him biting me. My experience of fighting with my sisters had taught me to fear the human bite, which is well known to have more germs in it than an average toilet or a dog's bum, whichever is closer.

But it was too late to go back now.

The door opened.

I pounced.

I grappled.

I got up.

I spoke.

'Sorry, Spam, I thought you were the Phantom.'

'You didn't have to bite me!' moaned Spam.

'It wasn't a bite. Your hand just got accidentally trapped in my mouth. Don't tell anyone, will you?'

'No. But you owe me a packet of crisps and a Mars bar.'

'Normal or king size?'

'Normal will do.'

'Deal.'

We shook on it.

We hung around for a few more minutes.

'Don't reckon the Phantom is going to show up,' said Spam.

'Me neither. We probably scared him off.'

We were on the stairs when Spam started to look thoughtful. He was definitely one of those people who let you know when they are doing some serious thinking by furrowing their brow, stroking their chin, etc. etc. He was a terrible poker player – partly because he had trouble hiding his thoughts, but also because he kept getting poker mixed up with Snap, which is a completely different game altogether.

'Why did you decide to use the ground-floor bogs, Donut?'

'Because that's where the first attack occurred. While I was in the cubicle. And the Phantom would have followed me down there ...'

'But there's no reason why the Phantom would have to use the same toilet that you were in. As long as you're out of class, he could dump the, er, *dump* in any toilet. Like the one on the second floor . . .'

We looked at each other. And then we sprinted up the rest of the stairs and along the corridor. Spam beat me to the toilet and burst in, but I was right on his tail. And there, in the middle of the floor, was a four-inch poo: the calling card of the Brown Phantom. Of the scoundrel himself there was no sign.

'Curse that evil super-villain!' said Spam, a bit melodramatically, if you ask me.

'At least we've discovered it,' I said, looking on the bright side. 'Get some bog roll and clean it up before anyone else sees it and points the brown finger of blame at me.'

'What? Why me?'

'Toss you for it?' I said, getting my lucky 50p
out of my pocket.

'OK. Heads.'

I tossed.

'Oh, bum!' I said, and went to get a wad of
bog roll.

NOTE TO SELF: FIND A NEW
LUCKY COIN – THAT 50P
IS USELESS.

But all was not lost. At lunch, I asked Renfrew
about his mission. His job had been to slyly
observe the class after I left, to see if anyone had
acted suspiciously, particularly in a texty sort of
way. He nodded, looked in both directions to
make sure that no one was observing us, and

made a sound. It was a sound both ominous and actually quite funny.

The sound he made was '*Pfumpf*.'

DONUT COUNT:

Tuesday 30 January

We had another War Council at break. Not
the full War Council, because that would have
needed Jim and he wasn't there. Renfrew was
wearing his Sherlock Holmes hat, mainly, I think,
to be annoying.

ME: OK, gentlemen, let's summarize everything
   we know.
SPAM: Everything we know? That'll take *years*.
ME: Don't try to be funny, Spam, it's not your

way. I mean, everything about the Case of the Brown Phantom. And don't make me state the obvious again or I'll sit on you. Renfrew, kick us off.

RENFREW: After you left to go to the toilet because of your diarrhoea—

ME: I haven't *got* blinking diarrhoea! That was just my alibi for going to the bog.

RENFREW: Whatever you say. After you went to the toilet with your *pretend* diarrhoea, Corky nudged me and pointed at Ludmilla. She was rummaging around in her bag like she was looking for a pen or something. Then I realized that she was taking too long about it. And her fingers were moving in a way that they only ever do when you're texting.

CORKY: Sp-sp-sp-sp—

ME: Exactly, Corky – she's the spy. I made the

classic mistake of underestimating her because
she's basically a troll and I felt guilty about the
whole banana thing. It's like a Greek tragedy.

CORKY: Sh-sh-sh—

SPAM: Yeah, shut up about Greek tragedies and
get on with the detectoring.

ME: Fine. Just trying to raise the level. Anyway,
Ludmilla is the Betrayer, and now we know
that she'll lead us straight to the Phantom like
a guided missile. Maybe. Next, Spam, what do
you deduce from the incident in the toilets?

SPAM: The poo we discovered was definitely the
smallest one so far.

ME: Precisely. And that means?

SPAM: It was probably the last of the batch . . .

RENFREW: He's out of ammo!

ME: For now . . . but we have a window of
opportunity in which to act. I suggest a twin-

pronged attack, which history has proved
to be the most effective battle plan, apart
from just having millions more men and
totally swamping the enemy, or having loads
of massive bombs. And sadly both of those
methods are beyond our reach. So, our next
move?

RENFREW: We interrogate Ludmilla.

ME: Agreed.

SPAM: And maybe put Chimpsters Zoo under
surveillance?

ME: How the heck do we do that? It's an hour
and a half away by car.

SPAM: Ah . . . I don't really know . . .

ME: Well, when there're two things you could
do, and one of them is practically impossible,
then logic suggests that we should do, like, the
other one. That right, Sherlock?

RENFREW: Sure is!

SPAM: Did you know that if you're in the
middle of drinking some milk, and you sneeze
and hold your nose at the same time, the milk
will come out of your eyes?

EVERYONE: Shut up, Spam!

DONUT COUNT:

Wednesday 31 January

There was no opportunity today to 'talk'
to Ludmilla. At morning break, Mr Fricker
summoned me to his office. He put his finger
to his lips, indicating that I should shut up. Then
he put on a fan, which whirred like a Spitfire
propeller.

'Walls have ears . . .' he said.

I shrugged. The whirring fan meant that we
had to shout so that we could hear each other,
which made it a bit futile really, given that

absolutely anyone in the gym would be able to hear us. But I thought it probably wasn't worth pointing this out to Fricker in case he put his Ninja Assassin hands on.

'The clock is a-ticking, Millicent,' he confided loudly. 'I can't keep them off your back much longer.'

'I'm working on it. We have some leads . . .'

'Leads are no use to me. I need something concrete to show to the Chief. What can you give me?'

'Just this: the truth is a cruel mistress – she smiles with one hand and kicks your backside with the other.'

'Millicent?'

'Yes, sir?'

'Get out.'

I told the gang about the clock ticking/sand-running-out business at lunch time. Lunch, by the way, was fish fingers. Sounds better than it was – you cut your fish finger in half, expecting to see something white and fishy in there, but what you actually saw was a fibrous mess exactly at the mid-point between grey and brown.

'What kind of fish is browny-grey?' said Spam, staring at his with a scientific detachment that I admired.

'There's a kind of fish called a grayling, I think . . .' said Renfrew. 'And if that mated with a brown trout . . .'

None of us had much appetite after thinking about *that*. Frankly, you'd be weird if you did.

Weirder, I mean, even than Spam, Renfrew, Corky and me.

DONUT COUNT:

NO
donuts

Not deliberate – I've just had so much to think about that I plain forgot to get my hands on a donut. And now I'm regretting it. There's a donut-shaped hole in my stomach. So that's a hole with another hole in the middle of it, which is definitely the holiest kind of hole.

Thursday 1 February

It was Corky's idea to follow Ludmilla to the chip shop at morning break. We saw her squeeze through the hole in the fence and stump across the no-man's-land to reach the streets outside the school. I knew it would take all four of us to tackle the Pfumpster. It was like something my dad

had told me about the Second World War. The Germans had miles better tanks – e.g. the mighty Tiger and the even more excellent Panther, not to mention the much feared Tiger II. Anyway, you'd need at least three Shermans to even think of taking on a Tiger, and even then you might all get your turrets blown off. But four on one and you had a decent chance, although you had to put a shell in the Tiger's vulnerable rear.

That was our best hope with Ludmilla.

NOTE TO SELF: AVOID REFERRING TO THE TIGER
TANK'S VULNERABLE REAR, IN CASE PEOPLE THINK
YOU MEAN LUDMILLA'S BUM. WHICH YOU DON'T.
I HOPE.

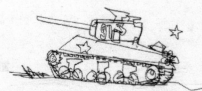

We cornered her after she came out of the chip shop. She had the bag in one hand and a wooden fork in the other. I wasn't sure how much damage she could do with that fork. It would probably break if she tried to stab you in the heart with it, although it might work in an eye-gouging capacity.

'Hello, Ludmilla,' I said, trying not to think about her jabbing the fork into my eyes.

'Pfumpf,' she replied dismissively.

'I thought we had an understanding, Ludmilla.'

'Pfumpf.'

'I thought we were . . . friends.'

'Pfumpf, pfumpf.'

'OK, Ludmilla, you want to play hardball. One of my associates quite clearly saw you send a text when I went to the toilet the other day.

And straight—'

'Because of your diarrhoea,' chipped in Renfrew unhelpfully.

'*I haven't got blinking diarrhoea!!!* Where was I? Ah yes . . . and straight away the Brown Phantom appeared to lay his dastardly thingy on the toilet floor. And that's no more of a coincidence than the cabbage smell that follows one of Corky's farts.* So that means that you're just as guilty as the Phantom and you'll be in just as much trouble. Unless you confess it all to us now, in which case there's a chance of a plea bargain.'

'A what?' said Spam.

'Shut up, Spam,' I hissed back.

Then I saw what was happening to Ludmilla's

---

* The loud ones, that is. The quiet ones are usually eggy.

face. It was crumpling, and then re-forming and crumpling again, as if she was desperately trying to control it – I saw this thing once where someone was trying to make a dish on a potter's wheel, and it was hilarious because the clay just went all over the place, and the harder they tried to make it go into a dish shape, the more it looked like an explosion in a jelly factory.

'I'll never betray him!' she cried.

'Eh?'

'The one you call the Phantom. I . . . I love him!'

'No need for that sort of language,' I said.

I hadn't expected this reaction. Not from the Pfumpfster. I suppose the reaction I expected was more of a 'Shut up, you stupid pudding, or I'll ram these hot chips in your fat face.' Also, well, I was a bit miffed. I mean, Ludmilla was supposed to be in love with me, wasn't she?

'You don't know what you're saying,' said Spam. 'The Phantom is evil. Pure evil. You've got to tell us who he is.'

Then Ludmilla uttered a strange, high-pitched cry and launched herself at me. It was like being hit by a charging rhino and I went down with her on top of me. I was pinned there, and she grabbed hold of my ears with her hands and started to pull my face towards hers. It was clear to me in that moment that she planned to bite my nose off.

But I remained reasonably cool under the circumstances. In between a certain amount of begging for mercy, I managed to say to the guys (who were, after the initial shock, trying to wrestle her off me), 'Get her bag. Her mobile. See who she texted . . .'

That had an immediate effect. Ludmilla

leaped off me and snatched the bag back from
Corky, delivering a vicious slap while she was at
it, which sent Corky reeling, and he is not the

sort of kid to reel easily. Then she plunged her hand into her bag and pulled out her mobile. Which she then proceeded to EAT!!!!

Well, not *eat* as in swallow and digest, but eat as in take big bites of it, which she then spat out and ground into the floor with her foot. I suppose she got the idea from my banana stunt, which had put the whole idea of eating things best left uneaten on the agenda, not to mention the menu.

We stood around, faintly amazed at this performance (except Corky, who was still too busy reeling).

'You shouldn't really do that,' said Spam, after a while. 'Mobiles have poisonous stuff in them. Mercury. Arsenic. Er, plutonium . . .'

'And all you really had to eat was the sim card,' added Renfrew.

It was almost sort of funny. But then I had one of my rare moments of human decency. I saw, like in a kind of vision, how the Temptation of Ludmilla must have happened.

And, like all the best moments of human decency, I knew how to use it to my own selfish advantage.

'It was like this, wasn't it . . . You were heartbroken because of the banana. The Phantom preyed on your weakness. He charmed you. He spoke sweet words, did he not?'

'Pfumpf,' she said, but it was more tearful than her usual noise. In fact, it was close to a sob. Making girls sob was well down on my list of priorities in life, coming under harpooning whales, clubbing seal pups, and snipping the ears off baby rabbits with gardening shears.

Except, of course, when it came to making

my sisters cry, which was quite a different matter.

'He made promises, didn't he . . .' I added, in a softer tone. 'Promises about what he'd do if you just let him know where I was? Seemed such a small thing . . . And I suppose he told you what a rat I was—'

'He didn't need to, *pfumpf*.'

'But it was all lies. I'm not a rat, *he* is. Just tell us who it was . . .'

'NEVER!'

And with that, Ludmilla broke through the human cordon and fled on her tree-trunk legs.

'Shall we go after her?' said Spam.

'Nah,' I replied sadly. 'I've seen enough misery for one day. We'll have to find some other way of striking back at the Brown Phantom.'

DONUT COUNT:

There are times when sadness consumes the human soul . . . and so the human soul gets its own back by consuming something else.

Friday 2 February

I had to buy more time. There was only one
way to do that. I had to go right to the top. That
meant Mr Steele, the headmaster.

Right at the beginning of the first term,
he had told us in assembly that, 'My door is
open, always open, to any boy or girl. Or any
other kind of person. Indeed any human being,
regardless of colour, sex, species or, ah, shoe size.
All you have to do is knock, and that open door
shall be, er, shall be, that is to say . . . opened

223

even more. Opened up to the hilt.'

So at morning break I went up to his office. Miss Bush lived in a sort of mini-office that you had to go past to get to the headmaster's.

'Where are you going?' she asked in her piercing voice. She didn't seem like a very happy person, Miss Bush. I suspect that she was Wronged in Love as a young woman. Maybe it had involved some confusion over a message written on a banana, although I admit that that would be a pretty big coincidence.

'I need to speak to Mr Steele. It's urgent.'

'I'm afraid you can't see him.'

'Oh, isn't he in?'

'Yes, he's in, but he refuses to see people when he's in. He's very specific about it.'

'Oh. When *can* I see him?'

'You can try when he's out. He left no

instructions about not seeing him when he isn't here.'

'So, when he's in I can't see him, but I can when he's not here?'

'That's it, yes.'*

'But that's just silly.'

The look she gave me discouraged further discussion. If I'd been communicating via banana, the banana would have said, 'No wonder you were unlucky in love: you're horrible and slightly mad.'

I walked away, waited a minute, and then crawled across the floor, commando-style, past her room. On the way, a teacher called Mrs Akimbo

---

* I believe that Mr Steele got the idea for this from a book called *Catch 22*, rather than thinking it up for himself, which is actually quite lazy and probably counts as plagiarism.

stepped over me without pausing, probably thinking that I'd fainted and that someone else would deal with me sooner or later.

I reached Mr Steele's door and got to my feet. Commando-style crawling is actually quite tiring, so I waited a minute to get my breath back. I could see the shape of the headmaster through the frosted glass.

I knew that, at any moment, Miss Bush or even Mr Whale might see me, and then I'd never get the chance to put my case to the Head. So I took a last deep breath, knocked and, without waiting for an answer, barged straight in.

Mr Steele seemed to be stabbing himself in the nose with a pair of scissors. Then I realized that he must be trimming his nose hair. Odd that he should be vain about his hairy nose but not his hairy ears. Anyway, his eyes opened wide in astonishment, and he pulled the scissors out of his nose and flung them in his desk drawer.

'I never touched the woman. Or the money. It was a simple misunderstanding. My finger became caught in the fabric, and— Oh, are you a whatsit, pupil?'

'Yes, sir.'

'Not connected to the police or security services in any way?'

'No, sir.'

I couldn't help but notice that Mr Steele's shirt was buttoned up all wrong and his tie was twisted round to one side. Despite his great age, he looked more like a scruffy schoolboy than a teacher.

'How did you get in here?' he said in a baffled way. 'I left instructions that I'd only see people in my absence . . .'

'Miss Bush said to come right in.'

'Bush . . . in . . . right . . .' Mr Steele seemed to be having difficulty grasping the meaning of my words.

'Sir, your open door . . . You spoke about it. Said we could come to you if we had any problems.'

'Precisely. My door is always, ah, *agape*. So long as I don't have to be on the other side of it. Burdens of office . . . uneasy lies the head that wears the crown, many a mickle makes a muckle, and so on and so forth, ad infinitum.'

Mr Steele gazed into the distance, haunted, perhaps, by the idea of infinity he had just invoked.

I didn't know how to begin, so I waited a

moment. He focused on me again, and looked a little startled.

'So what is it I'm supposed to do for you? Come on, boy, haven't got all day. A rolling stone waits for no man.'

'Right, sir. It's about the Phantom.'

'The what?'

'The Brown Phantom, sir.'

'The who?'

'The poo, sir.'

'What poo?'

'The poo that's been left lying around.'

'There's poo left lying around? Why was I not told of this? It is an outrage. We had toilet facilities installed so that such things would never happen again, not in my life time. We all remember the Great Stink of 1972. Well, I vowed that I'd make history a thing of the past.'

'I think you were, sir. Told about it, I mean.'

'Then I shouldn't have been. I am not the sort of Head to become bogged down in such matters. I have higher policy . . . the curriculum. The . . . the . . .'

'Sir, I just wanted to say that I think I know who's behind it—'

'Behind? No, that's not how it works at all. You have to be in front of it. If you're behind it, you've probably already stepped in it, and that, I can tell you, is no way to start a picnic.'

I ploughed on, determined to drive that particular image out of my head.

'But I need another few days, sir, to finish my investigation.'

'A couple of days? Fine. Rome wasn't burned in a day. Or a couple of days. And when in Rome, do as you would be done by. Although

I wouldn't advise turning the other cheek. Not in Rome. Especially in those alleyways around the . . .' A shudder passed through the Head.

'Right, sir. So you'll let him know?'

'*Him?* Who? This Brown Phantom of yours? They seek him here, they seek him there . . .'

'No, sir. Mr Whale.'

'What? Mr Whale has been leaving dirty doo-doos around the school? Well, I'm disappointed but I cannot say that I'm surprised . . .'

'No, sir. Mr Whale isn't the Phantom. You have to tell Mr Whale to let me have a few more days so that I can find out who the Phantom really is.'

'Ah, I see. Yes, I'll send him a memo. Not quite sure what a memo is, but I'll send him one. Do please send Miss Bush in as you leave. She'll know what a memo is.'

As I left, Mr Steele reached again for the scissors and went back to work trimming his nose hairs.

DONUT COUNT:

Saturday 3 February

I suppose it had to happen. Ella had her Goth boyfriend, so Ruby had to counter-attack by finding someone stupid enough to want to go out with her. He's called Brandon and he wears a hoodie and his acne is so bad, even his spots have spots. Ruby only went out with him to annoy Ella, which is fair enough, I suppose. My mum and dad like him even less than Crow. Brandon is basically a Chav, but we're not allowed to say Chav any more because it's racist or sexist or something.

I came in today and they were in the middle of a brilliant row.

It seems that Mum had banned Brandon from wearing his hoodie in the house. He said he could wear what he wanted, so my mum banned *him* from the house as well as his hoodie. I think that's probably for the best as there's a good chance one of his zits would burst and break a window, or hit someone in the eye and blind them.

Anyway, while Mum was telling Brandon that he was banned from the house, Ella and Crow were sort of hiding in the corner of the room, because everyone knows that Goths are frightened of kids like Brandon, on account of Goths being so easily broken because of their skinny legs and long fingers.

Well, the Goths may have been frightened of Brandon, but *everyone's* frightened of my mum, so Brandon decided to take it out on someone else. Crow was the obvious target.

'What are you grinning at, you *** *****?' he yelled. 'You should stay in the ***** zoo where you belong.'

Then my dad came out of the toilet and literally threw Brandon out, saying stuff about never showing his face round here again, while Ruby lay on the floor and wailed. And if she'd had a harpoon and some whales, she would probably have whaled as well.

All in all, it was about the best fun I've had in . . . well, almost the best fun I've ever had, despite the profound depth of human misery on display. But, as I've always said, there's hardly any situation in life that isn't made slightly better by the sight of your sisters being upset.

Anyway, about ten minutes later it sort of sank

in, the odd thing that Brandon had yelled at Crow. I think some deep and clever part of my brain must have been working on it in the meantime.

By this time, Ella and Crow had gone down to the bottom of the garden, past the smouldering pile of leaves that my dad kept burning for most of the year to annoy the neighbours. I think they went down there to snog and talk about which *Twilight* book was the best and where to get hold of good cheap eyeliner – that sort of Goth junk.

I didn't want to get too close, in case they were actually snogging. That would undoubtedly have made me splash my donuts on the fire, and roast donut sick is not, I'm guessing, a smell you really want to have in your nostrils.

So, staying on the other side of the smouldering leaf pile, I shouted out:

'Hey, Crow!'

His spidery form, wreathed in smoke, appeared out of the bushes. He moved his ridiculous index finger to indicate that he was listening.

'That idiot, Brandon, said something about you going back to the zoo. What did he mean?'

Crow considered briefly how he could convey his meaning with nothing but further finger gestures, but then gave up and spoke using his actual vocal cords. He sounded surprisingly like Shaggy from Scooby Doo. That was obviously the reason he communicated mainly by finger, 'cos you would, wouldn't you, if you sounded like Shaggy.

'Ice cream. I, like, convey it to the public. At Chimpsters Zoo. Or rather, I did . . .'

I was now quite excited. You know that feeling you get sometimes when you're playing cricket, and even before the bowler has bowled, you absolutely know in an almost supernatural and quite spooky way that the batsman (or batsgirl, if you're being forced to play with your stupid sisters on the beach) is going to hit a catch straight at you? And, armed with that knowledge, you can dive out of the way of it, because frankly only a madman (or madgirl if you're playing with your sisters) gets in the way of a cricket ball.

'What do you mean, you *did*?'

'I have been dismissed from their, ah, *employ* . . .'

'What for?'

'The circumstances were a little . . . *compromising* . . .'

'Don't talk to him,' hissed a voice from the bushes. 'He's an evil imp. An evil, fat imp.'

'Shut up, you,' I replied wittily. 'Anyway, how

can you get a fat imp? Imps are little. And they don't even exist. So your insult has absolutely no logic to it. And if he doesn't tell me, then I'm going to tell Mum and Dad that you've been snogging in the bushes.'

'You do that, you filthy beast, and I'll tell Mum all about your secret donut stash.'

'If you do that, I'll—'

'Hey, chill out, you two,' Crow said. ''Cos it is most seriously uncool what you're doing right now. I'll tell the little round dude what he wants to know. The thing is, some kid came up to me at the ice-cream stand. And, like, most kids want a 99 or a double cone with syrup and nuts and whatever, but this kid asks me if I can get hold of some stuff which is, like, the opposite of ice cream. And I said, "No way, kid," and he sort of flicks his fringe out of his eyes and he says,

"Name your price," so I say, "A hundred quid," thinking he'll just get lost and I can get back to scooping. But he doesn't bat an eyelid. He opens his wallet and peels out two twenties and a ten, and says I'll get the second fifty on delivery.'

'Hang on, just let me get this straight – he's asking you for poo, right?'

'Poo, yeah . . . How did you . . . ? But that's not the word he used.'

'And would the animal poo he wanted by any chance be from our nearest relation?'

'Your sister? No way. That would gross me out, dude. There's a line in the sand . . .'

Turns out Crow was that interesting subspecies, *Gothus stupidus*.

'I was thinking of the chimpanzee.'

'Hey, yeah, that's exactly, like, *it*.'

'And you got the chimp poo for him?'

'It wasn't easy, man. I had to slip a twenty to the guy who cleans out the cage.'

'And the kid, he came back for more?'

'He did. And the cage-cleaning guy said he wouldn't do it again, because, like, it was more than his job was worth as there are these laws about the things you can do with exotic animal, er, dung, and selling it to schoolkids is totally not one of those things.'

'So, let me guess, you tried to go in and get it yourself?'

'Yeah, that's it. I borrowed the overalls that the, er, dung guys wear, and I followed the team in. I managed to get a bucketful. But then the supervisor sussed me, and that was it. I got the sack, no second chance, nothing. All over a bucket of chimp dung. You know, if it was lion, then fair enough. But chimp – I feel like the punishment and the crime were most definitely not in synch.'

Then Crow came a little closer, looking back nervously over his shoulder. He continued in a confiding whisper, 'I really needed that ice-cream job, dude. Your sister, well, she's got expensive tastes. *Really* expensive. She likes to go to the movies and stuff . . . All my other girlfriends, well, they were just happy to lurk around looking gloomy, and you can do that for *nothing*, man.'

'Well, Crow, I think I can help you earn a little extra money.'

'Really? How?'

And I told him.

DONUT COUNT:

Sunday 4 February

It all went down in the late afternoon. It had
been planned like a military operation, but with
many fewer tanks and ground-attack aircraft.
So, I suppose if it really was a military operation
it would have been rubbish – definitely in the
bottom one per cent, although not as bad as
invading Russia, which always ends in disaster. In
fact, the best advice my dad has ever given me
is never to invade Russia, because, as he pointed
out, you only end up retreating through the

Horror of the Russian Winter, which is just about the worst kind of retreat there is, apparently.

Anyway, the drop was arranged for the path by the canal bridge. We chose that spot because it was right under a street lamp and we needed the light. Me, Corky, Renfrew and Spam were hiding behind the wall. Jim was standing on the bridge, doing natural boy-type things, such as whistling, spitting into the water, throwing stones at the ducks, etc. etc. He also had his mobile phone in his hand. Not that he was talking to anyone. That wasn't the plan. Plus, he had no credit left.

He was ready to film!

Crow was waiting on the path. In his pocket he had my dad's dictaphone. In his hand he held a plastic carrier bag. In the plastic carrier bag was something very unpleasant indeed.

You remember *Whose Poohs*? Remember the prize? Remember who won it? Well, I'd been storing my 'winnings' inside a Tupperware container in the freezer. I thought I might get something for it on eBay . . . Little did I know when I stored it there that the celebrity poo was one day going to save my bacon.

It was pretty tense behind the wall.

Would he turn up?

Would he take the merchandise?

Would Jim manage to film it?

Or would we all freeze to death before anything interesting happened?

I passed out the emergency rations – there was half a donut each, except for me. I got a whole donut on the grounds that I needed the energy for all the major thinking I was doing, plus I'd bought them anyway, and if anyone

wanted to complain then they should have
bought their own donuts – or, for that matter,
any other snacks they felt like, e.g. crisps, nuts,
sausage rolls, Scotch eggs—

'I hear something,' whispered Renfrew.

I swallowed what was left of my donut and
peeked over the wall. And there, just coming into
the circle of light cast by the street lamp, was the
Floppy-Haired Kid himself.

Well, who else were you expecting – the
Prisoner of Azkaban?

The tension was so thick you could have cut
it with a knife and spread it on bread, maybe
with some jam or honey – although personally
I'm not a big fan of bee puke, which is what
honey basically is.

The two figures nodded to each other.

'Hey, Steerforth,' said Crow, as arranged

beforehand. It was vital to get the Brown
Phantom's real name on tape.

'I said no names, you freak!'

'Chill out, man. You want the stuff or not?'

'You got it?'

'I got it. You got the money?'

The FHK reached into his pocket and took
out some notes and held them out. They made the
exchange. The FHK looked suspiciously at the bag.

'This definitely the same stuff?'

'I saw it come out of Samson with my
own eyes. He was reading the newspaper and
whistling *Dixie*. Check it if you want.'

The FHK began to open the bag, but then
thought better of it.

'OK, I trust you.'

'So what are you using this stuff for, anyway?'

'I've already told you – that's my business.'

'Look, I just need to know that it's legal. That you're not doing anything against the law with it. Otherwise I'd be an accessory, and I could be staring down the barrel of a long stretch in the pen.'

'Hey, it's not against the law to leave poo lying around on the floor at school—'

This was what I was waiting for. The FHK was about to condemn himself by means of his own evil mouth. But just then a terrifying scream rent the evening air.

'NOOOOOOOOOOOOO! IT'S A TRAP!'

I saw the huge, lumbering form of Ludmilla Pfumpf come pounding into view. I also saw the look on the FHK's face. It was a horror-and-bewilderment sandwich, smeared over with the mayonnaise of disgust.

'Right, boys, let's move,' I said.

We jumped over the wall. (OK, so I had a bit

of help from Spam, but no one ever said that jumping over walls was my speciality.)

The FHK now looked even more surprised. But he was one cool customer, and soon his face was back under control and he appeared as bored with the world as ever, as though getting caught with a load of fake chimpanzee poo that you were going to use to frame the local fat kid in revenge for his earlier triumph over you was a regular occurrence.

'Ah, if it isn't Humpty Dumpty falling off his wall. Oh, and all the king's horses and all the king's men as well. What a bunch of losers.'

While he was speaking, Ludmilla charged up and gave the fragile Crow one heck of a shove. Luckily, she pushed him against the wall and not into the canal, or else it would have been the end for Crow as it's well known that Goths can't swim.

Then Ludmilla stood between the rest of us and the FHK, bared her teeth and gave us a snarl.

'The game's up,' I said, talking to the FHK rather than Ludmilla, who didn't seem to be in the mood for calm discussions. 'We know everything, and we've got it all on tape. Crow was wearing a wire, and Jim up on the bridge over there was filming it all. YOU ARE THE BROWN PHANTOM! And you're going down.'

The FHK tried to maintain his cool, but you could see the edges melting.

'You've got nothing,' he said, and hurled the bag of celebrity poo into the canal, where it floated for a moment before sinking into the murky depths. An angler was in for a nasty shock one day. That was one brown trout you wouldn't want to fry.

'You still getting this on film, Jim?' I called up to the bridge.

'Everything,' Jim replied, and gave me the thumbs-up.

'Think how it looks . . .' I said in a reasonable tone. I was enjoying this and was quite happy to string it out for a bit. I also didn't want to antagonize Ludmilla in case she threw *me* in the canal.

'You're gonna get expelled for sure,' chipped in Renfrew.

'F-f-f-f-for sure,' echoed Corky.

I was expecting more backchat from the oily swine, and for a second it really looked like that's what he was planning. He glanced from face to face, still sneering his sneery sneer.

But the truth is, he couldn't keep it up. His mouth opened and shut a couple of times, as if he was expecting a sarky remark to come out all by itself. But nothing emerged. It was like when

you massively puke your guts up, and there's
nothing left to come out, not even the brown
watery stuff. Not even a burp.

And so the once proud Floppy-Haired Kid
sank to his knees on the dirty canal footpath,
put his face in his hands and cried. I'd say he
cried like a girl, but given that Ludmilla was

there, looming over us all like a deadly war mammoth,* it doesn't seem appropriate, and is, in fact, rather sexist.

And watching him there on his knees weeping like the world's biggest baby, my feelings changed. I'd been hating him really rather a lot since I'd discovered that he was behind the poo plot. But now I just felt sorry for him.

'Please don't tell the school,' he begged.

---

* As far as I am aware, no ancient tribe ever used the mammoth as an instrument of war, but if they had, no one would have been able to stand up to them. Unless they had war elephants. I'd actually quite like to see a battle between war mammoths and war elephants. I suppose the outcome would depend on whether the battle was fought in Africa, where the elephants would be at an advantage, or in the frozen north, where you'd have to back the mammoths. One day they'll clone a mammoth from a frozen one in Siberia, and then we'll be able to find out.

'If I get expelled my dad'll never forgive me, and then my mum and dad will get divorced, and my grandmother's ill, and she'll probably die, and if you don't tell I'll give you a hundred pounds.'

'Oh, shut up, will you,' I said, suddenly irritated by him again. 'I don't believe a word of it, and anyway it would serve you right. Well, not the bit about your granny dying, because that would be a shame for her, and it's not as if *she's* the Brown Phantom.'

'Each?' said Corky, which obviously wasn't one of his stammering words.

'What?' said me and the FHK together.

'Corky means the hundred pounds,' said Renfrew. 'Do we get a hundred pounds each or altogether?'

'I think each would be better,' said Spam.

'Definitely,' added Jim, who'd come and joined us by now.

'No!' I said firmly. 'We're not going to stoop to blackmail – that would make us as bad as him.'

'Technically,' said Spam, 'this is more bribery than blackmail . . .'

'It doesn't really matter if it's bribery or blackmail,' said Renfrew. 'We can't take it, because the whole point is that unless Donut finds out the true identity of the Phantom and tells the school, then he'll get the blame for it. So we've got to turn Steerforth in, and that's all there is to it.'

'Noooooo!' wailed Ludmilla, who we'd forgotten about for a while – as had you, I expect.

I looked at Ludmilla, and felt another one of those troubling pangs of sympathy for her, even though she'd totally betrayed me to my mortal enemy. Love is a cruel master, and those who are enslaved to it often do stupid, annoying and treacherous things. And it was then that the idea came to me. Again, I suppose my subconscious mind must have been chewing it over, because by the time it reached the front of my head it was fully formed and, if I say so myself, rather beautiful.

'OK,' I said, 'I won't tell the school that you are the Brown Phantom.'

This was followed by groans and tuts from the gang.

'You're mad,' said Jim. 'You can't take the rap for this twerp.'

The FHK looked up at me, his eyes suddenly dry. He couldn't stop that sly little smile coming back on his face, which was a mistake.

'But,' I continued, 'there is a price . . .'

'So you *will* accept the hundred pounds?' said the FHK, showing his meanness of spirit and smallness of mind yet again.

'Oh no. Money isn't everything. My price is that you have to go out with Ludmilla, like you promised her.'

Well, that wiped the smile off his face.

'WHAT?'

'You heard. And you'd better be a decent boyfriend, which means doing whatever she wants you to do, whether it's snogging, going to McDonald's, or just generally hanging out.'

I once read about some theory that says that the amount of happiness and unhappiness in the world are exactly balanced. That seems a bit unlikely – it would mean, say, me finding a donut every time someone else stubbed their toe, and the two things are totally unlinked, so how could it happen? But even if it isn't true in the cosmic sense, it was true on that footpath beside the canal. Just as the FHK's mood fell into despair, so Ludmilla's feelings soared skywards until they reached heaven.

'So, do you agree or not, then?' I asked.

The FHK made a kind of mumbling noise.

'Was that a yes or a no?'

Another mumble.

'WHAT?'

And then, in the quietest possible voice that was still detectible by the human ear, he said, 'Yes.'

'You swear?'

'I swear.'

And then Ludmilla Pfumpf took him in her strong arms, picked him up, and delivered a quite possibly fatal kiss to his mean lips.

It was the greatest moment of my life.

DONUT COUNT:

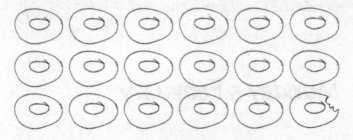

Oh, come on . . . I've wupped the Brown
Phantom's ass. What am I supposed to do to
celebrate – eat a carrot?

Monday 5 February

It was lunch time. I was in the headmaster's office. It was quite crowded in there.

There was Mr Whale, his baldy head and grim features making him look slightly more like an Angry Porpoise than an Evil Baby today.

There was Mr Wells, not quite knowing in which direction to beam his friendliness.

There was Mr Fricker, wearing his normal hands, although they were set in a position that made him look like he was strangling an invisible hamster.

There was Miss Choat, more ostrich-like than ever. If only a male ostrich would join the teaching staff, then perhaps her life of loneliness would be over.

There was Doc Morlock, mouth like a cat's bum, and, for all I knew, bum like a cat's mouth.

And, of course, as it was his office, there was Mr Steele, his hairy ears and his look of total bafflement filling up all the remaining space. When we'd first been shown into his office by Miss Bush, the Head bellowed, 'Abandon ship!' tried to escape out of the window and had to be dragged back by Mr Fricker.

I'd told my story to Mr Wells after morning

registration, and he'd arranged the meeting. He gave a quick outline of my story. Somehow, coming from an adult, it sounded even more ludicrous. That's the trouble with the truth – sometimes lies are so much more believable. Mr Whale was the first to respond:

MR WHALE: And you're seriously telling us
   that the person who's been leaving these . . .
   these . . . these . . . deposits—
DOC MORLOCK: Stools! Can we please call a
   stool a stool.
MR STEELE: Stools. *Mmmmmmmm.*
MR WHALE: Fine, stools. That these stools
   really belong to an ape at Chimpsters
   Zoo?
ME: That's it, yep, sir.
MR WHALE: And that someone at Chimpsters

was supplying these, ah, stools to a boy in this school?

ME: Yes, sir.

MR WHALE: And that you can prove that this boy wasn't you?

ME: I've given you the signed affidavit from the supplier stating clearly that it wasn't me.

MR WHALE: And yet this person cannot identify the true culprit?

ME: Like it says in the document, sir – the kid was wearing a hoodie. But he was skinny, and I'm definitely not skinny, so it can't have been me.

MR WELLS: Dermot has a point there, Mr Whale – no one would describe him as skinny.

MR WHALE: And you, Dr Morlock, can you confirm that it is possible that these *stools* came from a chimpanzee?

DOC MORLOCK: It is perfectly possible. Probable, even. A chimpanzee or a human who likes eating banana skins . . .

MR STEELE: Bananas.

MR WHALE: I don't know, I just don't know.

ME: Sir, it's really quite simple. Let me go over it again. Someone was out to get me, so they deliberately smeared poo around the place whenever they knew I wouldn't be able to prove exactly where I was. They'd heard about me eating that banana skin, so they realized that if they could get chimp poo, it would look like it was mine, although I just ate that banana skin because it had some embarrassing writing on it. The Brown Phantom got the poo from a guy who sells ice cream at Chimpsters—

MR STEELE: Ice cream*mmmmmm*.

MISS CHOAT: And what's to stop the Phantom from continuing his reign of terror?'

ME: He only did it to get me expelled. Now he knows that I'm in the clear, he won't bother any more. The days of poo in the corridors of power have gone.

MR WELLS: Well, that all seems clear enough. Dermot, get off to lunch.

MR WHALE: Not so fast. If the time you ate the banana skin in Mr Wells's class was the first and only time you've eaten a banana skin, then how come Dr Morlock identified the, ah, stool sample as belonging to you?

DOC MORLOCK: That is a point I would also very much like to have answered, Dermot.

ME: OK. Confession time. Those poo samples

I gave you last term, Doc, they weren't from me. They were from Samson.

MR STEELE: Samson?

ME: Yes, Samson – the big male in the chimp enclosure. I, er, got hold of some of his poo and pretended it was mine, Dr Morlock. Sorry about that, but I really didn't want to go to Camp Fatso . . .

DOC MORLOCK: I see. Well, you know, of course, what this means?

ME: I know, yes. You'll tell my parents and I'll be spending my next holiday in Camp Fatso.

MR STEELE: Fatso, fatso.

MR WHALE: Mr Fricker, what do you think of all this?

MR FRICKER: He did pass my lie-detector test . . .

MR WELLS: And he really hasn't got a bad
record at school.
MR WHALE: I think it has to be up to you,
Headmaster . . . Headmaster . . . ?

But when we all looked over to the
Head's desk we realized that he was no longer
there. We rushed over to the open window,
and saw that Mr Steele was already halfway
down the fire escape. At the bottom, he
kicked off his shoes and began to run across
the car park. As he ran, he tore off his jacket.
His shirt was next, and then his trousers. He
disappeared from sight, still wearing his vest
and underpants.

'You'd best go and collect him again, Mr
Fricker,' said Mr Whale. 'I suppose he'll be in
the dog-food aisle at the supermarket, as usual.'

Then he looked at me. 'Not a word, Milligan. Not a word.'

'No, sir,' I said, and I knew then that I was not going to be expelled.

Later on, in the schoolyard, I talked it over with the guys.

'But Camp Fatso . . .' said Spam, still unable to believe what I'd done. 'It's a living hell.'

'And you could have got that slithy tove out of our hair for ever,' added Renfrew.

We all looked over at the FHK. He was on a bench. Next to him, with an expression of bliss

on her face, was Ludmilla Pfumpf. As we watched, she bent her head towards his, and we saw Steerforth's eyes open wide with terror as she delivered another of her kisses. You could hear it go off like a hand grenade.

'But look how much happiness I've managed to bring into the world,' I said sweetly, and all the guys laughed, except for Corky, who let out one of his spectacular celebratory farts. 'And the thing is, I had a bit of a revelation back there by the canal. I'm twelve years old and I couldn't get over that stupid little wall without Spam giving me a leg up. That's totally rubbish. I'm too fat. No, no, don't contradict me. I am.' (Actually, nobody contradicted me.) 'Camp Fatso may be hell on earth, but it's only for two weeks, and at the end of it I'll be able to do all sorts of things that I can't do now. I'm going to come out a lean, mean fightin' machine. You wait and see.'

At that moment Tamara Bello appeared before us. Looking as cute and as haughty as ever. I was expecting some sort of snooty put-down, but she handed me something.

'I heard what you did for Ludmilla. I thought it was . . . cool.'

I probably should have said something back, but I was too slow. She spun like a ballerina and walked away on her tiny pointed feet.*

I looked down. There was a banana in my hand. Something was written on it in a rather elegant script.

It said:

* Feet are, of course, the best things for walking away on.

ANTHONY McGOWAN

THE BARE BUM GANG
and the The Holy Grail

Ludo, Noah, Jamie, The Moan, and
Jennifer are THE MIGHTY **BARE BUM
GANG!** Well, OK, not *that* mighty, but
they are about to face their toughest
challenge yet.

*An old tramp begs the gang to save his
mysterious treasure from an abandoned
block of flats. Standing in their way are
ruthless security guards, a terrifying
tunnel of doom and a vicious dog that is
almost certainly Zoltan, Hound of
Dracula.*

**Could the tramp really be King Arthur
reborn? Could his treasure be the
fabled Holy Grail? Probably not, but
anything is possible ...**

9781862303898

ANTHONY McGOWAN

THE BARE BUM GANG
and the Valley of Doom

Ludo, Noah, Jamie, Phillip and Jennifer are
THE BARE BUM GANG! They may have
a silly name, but they have an extremely
cool den, defended by kick-ass traps.

But now the gang are in desperate trouble, am-
bushed deep in enemy territory.
How can they possibly escape? And who
is the mysterious boy who helps them?

Things spiral out of control and Ludo finds himself
expelled from the gang. Will he
really join their ancient enemies to get
his revenge on his old comrades?

Find the answers in the awesome new
Bare Bum Gang adventure.

9781862303881

ANTHONY McGOWAN

THE BARE BUM GANG

and the Football Face-off

Meet Ludo, Noah, Jamie and Phillip –
THE BARE BUM GANG!

*The gang's new name is bad enough,
but things are about to get much worse.
Their number one enemies have challenged
them to a football match, and the prize at
stake is the gang den. And guess what –
THEY'RE ALL COMPLETELY RUBBISH AT
FOOTBALL!*

**How can they save the den? How can
they get back their pride?**

*Find out in the first
Bare Bum Gang adventure!*

9781862303867

ANTHONY McGOWAN

THE BARE BUM* GANG
battle the Dogsnatchers

Ludo, Noah, Jamie, Phillip and Jennifer
are **THE BARE BUM GANG**! They have
an embarrassing name but a cool
Gang Den, so things could be worse.

*The newest member of the gang is
Rude Word, the world's ugliest dog –
and he's causing trouble. He's throwing
up strange furry body parts . . . and
Mrs Cake's dog Trixie is missing! Ludo
and the gang have to turn detective and
get to the bottom of this gross mystery.
But when other pets disappear,
they realize the mystery is bigger
than they'd thought.*

**Can they get Rude Word
off the hook?**

9781862303874

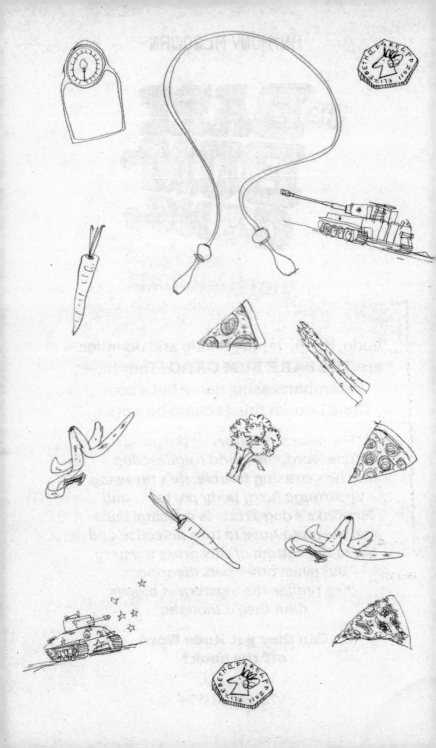